ELEPHANTS ARE NICER THAN WE ARE

Roy Stevens

ISBN 978-0-9556951-0-0

Printed and bound in Great Britain
First published in Great Britain in 2008 by Roy Stevens

Three people, hitherto unknown to one another, are exceptionally sensitised, partly as the result of neurological changes following a missile strike, to global cruelty and suffering. Their attempts to alert society to much that is unrecognised are met with incomprehension and hostility. They are eventually exiled as threats to society whilst they defend their "compassionate pessimism" against political, commercial, educational and religious opinion. They conclude that the "developed world" is still stone-aged beneath its civilised veneer.

This disturbing novel touches upon some of the author's own concerns, for world peace, respect for animal life, and for the arts, music especially. But basically this is a love story about the growth in relationship between a group of idealists, and their attempts to evade forces of oppression as they are watched, warned and eventually thrown out of their native land.

Roy Stevens was educated at schools in Bradford, London, and Lewes, and at Christ's College, Cambridge, where he took a double first in English.

My warm thanks are due to Brenda Ellis, patient and sorely-tried secretary-cum-typist, and to Lizzi Linklater's so helpful writing group at the York Central Library.

I am also grateful to Dr. Sophie Nicholls for opening up the route towards publication and for support throughout. Not least I must pay tribute to my family, who have endured "the book" for so long, my daughter, Penny's, skill on the computer being one of many ways in which home has always been at the centre of my world.

Roy Stevens,
New Earswick. York.

man, proud man!
Dress'd in a little brief authority –
Most ignorant of what he's most assured,
His glassy essence, -- like an angry ape,
Plays such fantastic tricks before high heaven
As make the angels weep.

<u>Measure for Measure</u>
2,ii

PART 1

SHOCK

(1)

It seemed like the Big Bang, the start of things. But at other times like later shocks, the shock of being born, being sent away from home, losing Rosie.

He had no idea where he was, and slipped in and out of consciousness. But in spite of the pain in his head, and the wounded feeling in his side, and the sharper agony of legs which were recognisable only as a pain somewhere, somewhere below, there was, intermittently, something else: a separate, utterly incongruous impression, a pleasure (even) in being able just to exist, without pressure, something which he had not experienced in twenty years of life: as if he had total free experience at last and required no other. Oddly he was in control. After the first shock, and all the others, up to this last, there would be no more. This now was rest, perhaps the last rest.

From time to time he was aware of white-coated figures beside the bed, and sometimes others in other uniforms, but he was unable to make sense of them or speak, and he would drift off to rest again.

One of the uniformed figures would sometimes lift him, wash him, make him sanitary. Why this person should bother he could not decide.

Once there was another faint shock, a shadow of that last: and once, though he didn't recognise a television screen, he heard something suggestive of noise and destruction. Again he suddenly remembered Rosie, his old dog, who disliked loud noises.

Occasionally there were other sounds, cries from somewhere near.

And then one day the full horror of what he had seen as flashes came upon him, and more of his own memory. Not just Rosie, leaving mother, the blow to the head. He realised that he had seen the distant past, and the future. This was the worst shock of all. He tried to rise in the bed, but could not, gasping for breath. Someone came and settled him down.

He came to be aware of other things, doctors who were talking about him, the occasional wail of a siren, and a woman who was often in attendance, usually at night. There seemed to be a quietness, an ease, about this woman, an emotional climate unlike that remembered from school and university, and from the demands of his own father. He began to want to tell her about the things he now knew, but could not speak.

The medical staff were grateful to her, as to many others, for help during the bombing. The young doctor in charge of the case was determinedly cheerful, smiling, though showing signs of strain. "Are you sure you're OK? I believe you've been having a rough time yourself."

"Yes. I've been out in Africa as a medical missionary...." She hesitated .... "But I got some funny tropical disease and they sent me home. A few weeks in a specialist hospital. But I'm clear now, and glad to help." She paused. "I'm not going back."

The doctor sensed that there was more to be told, but he added, "You seem to have a good effect on your patient. He's calmer when you are there, even though he's not speaking."

"Will he speak?"

"Difficult to say. The blow on the head was a serious one. He'll walk again in due course, but probably only with sticks.

There was a hint of kidney damage. A rotten bad case, like so many others."

"I feel that he's trying to say something."

"Nurse, keep up the good work."

One day she decided, with the doctor's encouragement, to attempt the therapy of her own speech. He was moved into a private room where she could speak clearly without causing disturbance.

He had slept a lot during that day, and seemed newly alert in the evening.

She was, however, nervous.

"My name is Elsa. I've been in Africa as a medical missionary. But I became ill, and I'm glad to help out here."

His eyes quickened. He was attentively listening. How much he understood she did not know.

What she did not fully know was the easement of her quiet voice and unaggressive manner.

"I was brought up rather strictly by my evangelical father, who ran an independent chapel. I just remember with gratitude my loving mother, who died when I was eight. Father didn't re-marry, and I was his only family."

She hesitated. His look seemed to say, "Go on."

But she could not. And he was not the reason.

After a moment, she said, "You are going to get better, and I am going to help you."

He was desperate for speech, to tell her all he had seen and known, so much more than the story of his own life. It would shock her: there had been too many shocks. For them both.

Towards daylight, a very few days later, she heard it. "Elsa." It was whispered, and it was hoarse, but he had spoken. She took his hand, and found herself in tears.

(2)

Day by day he found more words. She knew he was Robert, or Rob. She named him, and he repeated it, the shorter version. The doctor was delighted. There had been another explosion fairly near, which had set the patients back a little, but, said the doctor, "He's making such progress, and needs quietness, so we'll send him to an annexe a little out of town. That last bombing fortunately claimed no lives, and for the moment we can spare you, Elsa. I think you should go with him. We'll bring you back if we're desperate." The consultant was to visit him and maintain contact.

The cleaner air, the peace, and the view of green fields from Rob's room, together with the company of the nurse he knew and trusted, further hastened his recovery, and he was soon in a wheelchair. One sunny afternoon while she was pushing him round the well-kept garden, she realised that he was forming sentences, and, most thankfully, that as far as she could calculate, he was coherent, logical: perhaps there had been no irreversible brain damage. He said, "Tell me more about your life." He was trying to come to the double secret he could hardly bear to keep to himself.

She continued, expanding a little on aspects she had described before: then, hesitated. "I told you about my preacher father's being widowed. We had a housekeeper. My father and I were very close.

I was expected to show a godly example at his parade services, 'Affirmation Days' they were called. Dressing up, and taking part in a procession of witness through the streets, accompanied by a small band, and all of us in a kind of uniform with a text on the back. I hate to think of that now."

She hesitated again, uncertain as to the wisdom of going to the depths, uncertain as to whether, after the trauma he had suffered, a shared distress might weaken him, or strengthen their therapeutic relationship. But he spoke first.

"You've changed. Since you came back from Africa."

A little put about, she acknowledged that. But he went on.

"Part of the change was to do with animals, wasn't it?"

She had never mentioned that. She gazed at him, amazed.

"Yes, that's true. But how do you know?"

His eyes were fixed on her in an intense scrutiny which, she knew later, conveyed a kind of hopeless, or near hopeless, love, but also something more. His eyes shifted towards the shrubs and tall flowers in nearby borders.

"I know everything," he whispered. "That's the trouble."

Suddenly he was weeping quietly. She handed him a tissue, aware that something extraordinary was taking place, and also knew that some sort of bond between them had been made.

After a moment he said, "I know about your father, too. The shock you had. Why, after the training, you went abroad. Our whole world is a mass of shocks, bangs, explosions. Why can't we live and let live? But we never will – I know! The animals, wiser, do!"

They were passing a small garden summer-house. She drew the chair within, and sat down, close.

Tremblingly, she said, "You know he assaulted me? When I was fifteen. The house-keeper was away."

"Poor devil," Rob said. "He was probably desperate. No wife. No mate. A strict moral code. Poor devil."

For a moment she was furious. "He hurt me! And afterwards I had no one. We had few friends. And I was too shocked to tell. I just went away, and wept."

Now she was crying again.

He put an arm out to touch her. It was the first time she had seen him use that arm.

"Forgive me, forgive me. When you see it all – you see all ways."

Moved by the gesture of touch, the first which was not clinical, she bent over and lightly kissed him. For a moment no more words passed between them.

Then he said, "I have to tell you. I have to tell someone. But some will think I am mad. If they do, will you stand by me?"

Tear-stained still, she said, hardly understanding, "Of course I shall stand by you always." And mutual love was born. But this was to be no light romantic tryst.

He bent a little towards her. He was swiftly recovering, she noticed.

"Something happened when I was blown up. Thrown first against a shop, and then broken fencing, because a suicide bomber had made so many of us pay for his beliefs. Something happened because of the blow on the head. I was just an ordinary chap before. I rebelled against my army father, went to uni, where I wasn't likely to be brilliant. I had begun to – question – things. But afterwards...."

She held his still wounded hand more tightly. "Elsa, my nurse, my healer --- my best friend.... I began to see. Oh, my God, what is the use....?"

"I want to hear," she said.. "Please go on. I'm with you."

"When I began to come round in that hospital bed – though 'come round' isn't right – I could see, in my mind at first, only a great darkness; and then another explosion, a big bang. Call it a dream if you like. I believe I was seeing the beginning of all things – the primal things. I couldn't see beyond it, to see beyond time – I wished I could – it was cruel to deny me that! But I knew that from that primal spot of something unknowable came all the universe, and many universes, splintering out into infinite space; that stars, galaxies, suns, nebulae, all came from that first big bang, and that though there were to be millions, billions of light-years to come, space was to become ever vaster. I couldn't hold such emptiness. I knew that our sun, with its litter of planets round it, our Earth, was an inconspicuous star amongst millions of others within a vast galaxy, thousands of light-years across, and yet that galaxy was to be only one of many, so many! And suddenly I felt lonely. So lonely!"

Her grip upon him gently tightened.

"You could, so far, put it down to the dream of a wounded man, recalling, perhaps, detail from a science book for boys. But it went on. It sort of changed. The loneliness was added to by a sense of futility, that nothing at all was worth anything in the midst of all this, including wars and bombs and all unkindness. I think at this point I wished to be dead. But the worst was to come. The focus shifted, and I was seeing our little tiny pathetic Earth, ravaged by wars and tumult, and competing religions, and struggles for prestige and money, and I heard, as a kind of ground-bass, a moaning, a cry which was the perennial suffering of wounded things. Worse than everything was the vision – God knows how many or how few years ahead - of our own planet, with its soil, its sea, its good air, its rivers, forests, ruined and bereft of life forever. All that evolution, all evolution lost! And again I didn't want to live, not in that mess: couldn't bear to hear that suffering cry, and then see the disaster to come.

"And, Elsa – this is both marvellous and horrible. When I came to and saw you at the bedside, I knew that you, too, in some way, had recently been disillusioned, wounded: that we could understand one another."

She caressed him. There was silence.

Then she said, "I do not think you are mad. I think you are a good man. I will always stand by you. Later I'll tell you more; though there's not a lot to tell – about my own story into - I will not call it despair. There must be some way of using our faith, our unfaith, to help: something positive, constructive. Even if it's only half-true."

For a moment he showed real anger. A good sign, she thought. He is recovering. "You don't really believe me."

"I do," she cried. It was from the heart rather than from the brain, but sometimes the heart is right. "And I want to use it, use the despair."

His eyes lost their anger, brightened. "Will you help me?"

"Of course, love, of course." It was the first time she had used that, the word. But after all that had gone on she knew that she loved this man, that he loved her, this poor crippled thing. He might not be able to make love, even raise an erection. Who knew of these things? But they were bonded.

He steadily gained strength. His normal consultant came over, was pleased, checked him, and promised he would be walking within weeks. The new resident doctor was a different matter. A brilliant, brash extrovert, he soon gathered that his patient was under more than a physical cloud, became suspicious, and began to probe. Elsa thought Rob's room might have been bugged. The whole country was now in a high fever of worry about terrorist attacks, and long-standing safeguards as to the liberty of the individual were being discarded one by one: that included occasional searches of hospitals. Rob now kept a journal and was careful to conceal it well. Even so, it got about that the crippled man in number five was some sort of prophet and even a teller of fortunes. Once another patient came to ask for guidance, and was quickly turned away.

Elsa was now on day duty. Rob was felt OK to be left at night, barring emergencies. Even so she slipped in often. Once she asked to see his journal, and was gladly given it.

When he returned from an early bath one morning he knew at once that his room had been entered, drawers turned over.

The doctor came, suggesting a tranquilliser.

"No need."

"But you are worried, and stress may slow down or even reverse physical recovery."

"No need."

"Nurse, do you not agree with me?"

"I'm sorry, doctor, but I think Rob is managing well as things are."

"'Rob'? I hope you are not getting too familiar with your patient. That might prejudice proper judgement."

They got him away, but it was a struggle. "You called me Rob. I liked it."

"It came out without my thinking. I'm glad you don't mind. I'll go on being as professional as old Bossy Boots wants, but....we are, sort of mates, aren't we?" It was the nearest so far to an outright profession of love.

"What about the journal?"

"I was so moved to hear about the tussle between your mother and father when you were first sent away to school at eight years – when your mother pleaded that you should not go: and father, the army man, wanted you to be toughened up. How you didn't know then that your mother had lost another son. How she had wanted to keep you a little longer."

"Yes, and then I got a fever during that first term, and was sent home to recuperate. This time mother would not let me go. She was ill by this time. Without meaning to, I broke mum and dad apart. Not that I think they had ever been really happy together."

"It was another shock," said Elsa, "another tearing-apart. Like the severed arms and legs in these bombings. Like these, it was unnecessary." She cried, and held him tightly.

Another day when the first walking with sticks had gone well, the resident doctor came up.

"I think it would help things along to give you a series of anti-depressant injections," he said, smilingly.

"Never!" Rob cried.

"Please, no," Elsa again urged.

"My dear, you are only a nurse, and should not interfere."

She was standing between the two men.

"I shall have to report you to the Director," the doctor said, and strode out.

(3)

Less concerned to protect herself than to protect her man, Elsa thought much about escape from hospital. One senior nurse was a distant friend from training days.

She decided to approach this friend. With this risky procedure came more warmth than she had expected. The old colleague knew of rumours about Rob. She also had the resident doctor well in focus – "a clever cuss, but with the sensitivity of a brain-damaged rattlesnake. We don't like him. I suppose you'll try to leave with your patient?" A slight raising of the eyebrows. "I shouldn't worry too much about the Director. You are highly thought of, and she has problems of her own. The snag is that under all these regulations no one can discharge themselves. Checks and searches are the order of the day".

They were talking companionably over a cup of tea. "If you were on duty, could you 'not see us'? It's a lot to ask."

"I don't know, love. I need my job. My man's just left me."

"Please –"

"I can't let you out by this door."

"I don't mean now. But if you can think of anything."

Her friend softened. "I'd like to help; I know true love when I see it. Ask me again. I'll have a think. You'll stay with Rob?"

"Always," Elsa replied.

One night Rob woke screaming in the early hours: he had been through a violent nightmare, influenced by unpleasant images on television the previous evening.

Elsa came running, and several other patients were disturbed. The Deputy Director joined Elsa at the bedside and held him to try to ease his half-screams, half-weeping. "It was my mother," he sobbed. "She had been terribly wounded in a bombing, but she was pregnant, and there was a dead child. I tried to go to help, but I could not reach her. Oh, my God!"

For once he accepted a sedative, and Elsa lay beside him until he fell into a deep sleep.

The doctor was there promptly after breakfast. "I really think," he said, in his slightly sinister and enthusiastic way, "that this man is gravely disturbed. I stress again the advisability of treatment via injections. If he won't accept these, supported by you, nurse," - he looked with a hint of malevolence at Elsa – "then I think a short spell of specialist therapy in a mental ward would be indicated. Not for long necessarily," he added, as the other two reacted with dismay. "Just to assess things." He went on, "Some of his ideas are – let me put it mildly – a little dangerous. About not conceiving children, reducing populations, and all that."

Something in that last remark made Elsa suspicious. She chanced her arm, trying to rival his very direct manner.

"Have you been reading his journal?" She asked abruptly.

For once he was off guard. Reddening slightly, he replied, "I've looked into it once or twice, for security reasons."

She was furious. "You have burgled his room!" she screamed.

"We live in a very difficult time," he said, quickly recovering. "We have special powers. Some of his writing might be interpreted as criticism of our government. It might encourage revolt, even terrorism."

"Do you really imagine," still white with anger, she said, "that this wounded man who has seen and endured the effects of terrorism, might wish to encourage it? Do you thing he is an unfeeling robot?"

At last the patient spoke. "Doctor," he said, "you have grossly exceeded your rights. I want to get out of here."

"You can't," was the smooth, now cheerful reply in the tone of victory. "The Director and I must agree to your going. You might be a security risk, even unintentionally. Anyway, you are not fit to go yet."

"Please leave us," Elsa cried. And he went, briskly, gleefully.

(4)

"We seem to living in a new nightmare world," said Elsa.

"We shall get out. I know we shall," he replied, quietly.

He kept asking to see the hospital garden, which they loved. They spent more and more time there, in fine summer weather. When the Director came to visit them there, Elsa saw the gleam of a possible way out of their trap.

"He loves the fresh air, and flowers," she urged, "and often lies awake listening to the early birdsong. Since the bad nights he often wakes so early. Would it be possible to get him into the garden soon after first light, with the dawn chorus still on the go?"

The Director considered. "I love the garden myself, but I cannot give you authority to unlock doors so early in the day."

She added, after more encouraging talk about Rob's condition, that if a senior nurse was finishing a night duty, that person might have authority to give them the garden in the early morning.

On clinical matters, she was clearly downcast. "I don't like our resident physician's methods, not always, any more than you do. But I am only the Head of the hospital, and I have no final authority to disobey. He now has, as you know, certain special unidentifiable powers." She looked uncomfortable. "Fortunately your consultant tends towards your view of things. I will try and help," she said, rather disconsolately, as she left them.

Neither of the lovers had strong contacts in the capital. But on returning months earlier, from Africa, and after her time in hospital, Elsa had called to thank another member of her old missionary team, like her disillusioned, a friend who had been a support through Elsa's mysterious illness.

This young friend, Vicky, was not, like Elsa, a sort of rail-roaded evangelical Christian from a traditional family, but a wilder, very enthusiastic creature, from a fractured family life, always anxious to do good. After early years studying many creeds, she had for a time been bowled over by a peripatetic evangelist, a man, who, as she now laughingly admitted, converted people because of his mastery of gesture, a brilliant larynx, and a dramatically confident manner. She had gone through that phase hook, line and sinker, and come out of it as quickly. She once said, "Out there in Africa, he was getting people, he said, to God, but not bothering at all about apes turned out of the forest, and the whales slaughtered daily off the coast. I began to see through all this." She was now working in animal welfare, having seen that 'the animals have got it right – no bloody rule-book, just getting on with life.'

Elsa wrote to her. It was one of only a few life-lines. She had neither the time nor the inclination to try to find, at least in the first instance, a place of their own, and that would be less easy to conceal, if concealment was an issue, (might it be?) than a hiding-place with a friend or two.

She was suspicious of the telephone. An exchange of letters produced a plan to meet at a quiet tea-place in a nearby suburb. She was, she told hospital staff, using time off to get some clothes cleaned.

The two girls were well-contrasted. Vicky was tall, vividly clothed, with wild earrings, bangles, beautiful long dark hair. Not the sort Elsa had known in her religious missionary days with her father. Whereas Elsa was slim, of medium height, with short dark hair, still, as Vicky said, with the fragile beauty of a saint. At which they both laughed.

"Can you imagine me as a saint?" asked Elsa. "I was once a goody-goody, and my life was devoted to 'being pure'." I got it from poor old dad. He was utterly hung-up about purity. I once heard him give a sermon about purity to celebrate the installation of a new chapel organ! But look at me now – planning an illegal escape from a secure hospital with a man who people think is my lover. Might be," she added, with a drop of a tone.

Vicky was living with 'a great fella', Mick, an actor in an experimental theatre company, interested in radical, anti-government plays. "We might get raided," she added cheerfully. That was a possible snag. But Vicky had accepted with surprising ease all that she was told about Rob's prophetic gift. Elsa was glad to note that her friend, with her vital energy and enthusiasm, was likely to emphasise the positive side of non-belief in the future. "Let's all give each other a great, loving time," she said. That was to be a great need with regard to pessimism, – "Come and live with us."

The plan was delicately balanced. It needed fine weather. The friendly nurse who had wished to help the couple, but could not, now had authority to unlock the garden gate in the early morning when she was on duty. But there was a second key on the ring, which operated the lock of a back gate into a quiet lane. "It might be rusty," she added. "When I can, I'll slip out and oil it for you."

With fine weather needed to justify the lovers' early nature walk, the right nurse on duty, and a phone call to Vicky with her promise of a taxi: it was now a matter of waiting. Rob, who seemed to know, was confident of success. He presented a calm demeanour to the doctor, who was still planning something nasty.

At length after a period of rain and strong winds, came fine summer days. The senior nurse was on night duty, and it was planned to meet her at the garden door as she went off duty at seven. After opening the garden door she was to hand the keys over, so that

Elsa could unlock the back gate, then push Rob casually back round the lawn, and leave the keys where the nurse could find them.

The two runaways could then drift back towards the escape route, which was fortunately partially screened by bushes, leave the wheelchair somewhere concealed, and go. Rob could now walk with care a few yards to a newspaper-cum-grocery store where their taxi was to meet them. Their accomplice would be in the clear, with the keys replaced, and the fugitives' flight would remain a mystery.

That morning was beyond expectation beautiful, with birds singing for all they were worth, and the fresh scent of recently-mown grass. The lock was indeed well-oiled. With hearts pounding, they slipped out into the quiet lane. At the shop they bought a paper and some sweets. The taxi had not come on the dot, and not after five minutes.

The man remained composed, but Elsa was anxiously expecting the worst.

Vicky, with a heart of gold, was sometimes a little erratic and vague. Had she forgotten?

But then Elsa looked at Rob, so composed. Of course, he knew.

It came, ten minutes late. "Sorry, sir. Another bomb scare. Diversion." The driver helped Rob into the car, and their escape was complete.

PART 2

The Challenge

(5)

There was something unusual, highly-charged, about the atmosphere in the crowded concert-hall. The bomb scare, the relief felt after the all-clear, the general sense of living whilst threatened by an unknown enemy, and then the interval time to talk, unwind, joke, share worries: all this assisted to produce a performance of the last item with the *frisson* of a special excitement, a special commitment. Dame Emily felt it, as she so often felt when things were going particularly well, almost as one relinquishing control, trusting in the players: as if prepared for a new revelation of genius.

She had chosen a gentle and calming piece, one of her encores, as a lead into the interval. She hesitated about the advertised second half, but decided to let it stand.

The fourth, and last, symphony of Brahms is an epic work. Its elegiac first movement is marked by a conspicuous dip and rise theme, sombre in tone. The second introduces a sad, march-like tune in triple time, which alternates with an eloquent and wistful cello melody, later taken up by the full orchestra: this cannot not be a looking-back. The third movement seems to complete a view of life, much as the march does in Tchaikovsky's Pathetic Symphony – providing a boisterous, extrovert contrast with the darkness to come.

To those who do not know it, Brahms' last movement in symphonic form comes as a surprise. It might appear austere, academic only - thirty-two short variations in the minor key on a theme borrowed from Bach. It is bare, often uncompromising, and almost without relief, though it slips momentarily into a gentler, prayer-like sequence, before the relentless minor key returns, as if it were an inescapable fate, veering off-key itself for a moment only – as if to show that even fate cannot be depended on. The final variations invoke a sense of tremendous authority. Anyone coming freshly to classical music, and alarmed by the austere connotations of a theme with variations, might note in Brahms' achievement the union of the rigorously academic with the fearsomely human.

The eerie slow movement had evoked a silence in the hall almost audible. The extrovert third part was fun to hear, to conduct. But in the pause before the finale conductor and audience alike sensed the possibility of revelation, and one life-changing, but not as on the road to Damascus.

The attack on the last movement was precise: but Emily was unprepared for her sudden access of tears during the prayer-like passage in the major key – no one, she remembered, could make the brass sing as tenderly as Brahms could. She found herself thinking, too, of her young adopted daughter, rescued by some compassionate aid agency from the detritus of a foul inter-tribal war, and of the atrocities of that, and of all wars. As she raised the baton for the symphony's last devastating blows, a blackness swept over her. For a moment or two she was no longer conducting in a large concert-hall before many people.

In the silence, she stood rigid, baton in hand. The audience seemed as if suspended in a trance after a performance of unusual power. Some were in tears. Then when applause broke out, the conductor remained, as if unable to move. A couple of minutes passed before people realised that something was wrong. The applause began to die down. Then the Leader of the orchestra came forward, took the conductor's arm, and led her gently off-stage. He swiftly returned, brought the orchestra to its feet; then the applause was wildly renewed. One section after another was signalled for praise, the woodwind, the timpani, the cellos, the brass, as the audience's response became more confident at the display of normality. And then all the players rose once or, twice, until a sudden silence came over everyone as Dame Emily, with her personal assistant close behind, returned centre stage for a moment only.

"I do so much apologise for my odd display," she said, with a smile of sorts, "but great music has taught me something about life, as it has, I am sure for you too. I will say more later. Thank you for sharing this evening with us. Great art may yet find the truth hidden from leaders of men. Goodnight, and … look after each other." The last words came with a peculiar emphasis. She left the platform again.

Reassured that the much respected, well-loved leader was recovering, the clapping was renewed, with players brought to their feet. People did not seem to want to leave, but dispersed slowly, talking.

(6)

This was the autumn of the storm, and also of renewed bombing. It was a peculiar storm, more compact, more concentrated in its attack than the great storms which had increasingly been devastating much of the world. It skirted their city, but fell in all its intensity upon a stretch of coast eighty to a hundred miles distant, where caravans and poor hutments took up much of the beaches in front of the run-down, deprived industrial towns behind. A tornado or two, hitherto unknown, a new threat, tore down miserable tenements, long overdue for replacement, demolished a school, and laid low streets of poor terrace houses. Most dramatically, the spire of the parish church, a support and symbol of charity within a community where love seemed at a discount, fell across the church square into a supermarket where many had taken refuge. With power and lighting off, transport at a stop, and floods now sweeping in from the sea, and with many dead and injured, the nation took note of one more shock after so many in recent months at home and across the world.

It was brutal to bomb at this time. Bomb they did. Whilst rescue for storm victims was gathering pace, the capital was a target for terrorists, who struck at railway stations, a church, a barracks, and the Archbishop's palace, which might have been thought to be immune.

A wave of something like despair swept over the nation, as nature and moral evil combined to weaken faith in life. And by that token, the Archbishop, in normal times a moderate and mildly ineffective man, was to become an agency for change.

Whilst leaving the building with his dog to investigate damage, both had been struck by a falling pillar. He picked up his dog, now piteously crying with legs broken and a bleeding side, and, weeping, went within. His Chaplain found him sitting, the dead dog in his lap, gazing into space and, for the moment, incapable of speech. It was difficult to get medical help for him, but then his wound did not seem too serious. At length he was taken back to the study, where he sat, refusing bed, holding the dead dog and saying something like, "A change, a change. I must change."

(7)

The Chaplain, humble and deferential, went only so far. He had looked over the Archbishop's address.

"Do you not think, Your Grace, that you might postpone or cancel your next appointment? You have, after all, been involved in an accident, shocked, and injured."

His superior, with a plaster on the forehead, but otherwise seemingly alert and healthy, looked him in the eye. The reply came in a tone which to the Chaplain was new, definitive.

"Remember," he said, "that religion is a seeking, not a finding." Then he added, as if to himself, "If there is a separate thing called religion, or ought to be."

He was to preach on the Sunday following at a provincial cathedral forty miles distant, set in pleasant, relatively unspoilt country, a region of woodland and pleasant fields. "Can we go by train?" he asked. The Chaplain, glad to be away, hurried to see whether there was indeed a railway line, and a suitable train on it.

And so it was that instead of travelling in the normal limousine, the Archbishop arrived at a provincial railway station, having compromised with the tumult in his heart by travelling first-class.

He was offered refreshments before robing, whilst all around showed deference, sometimes obsequious. "How strange it all seems now," he reflected. But as yet he gave no outward sign of things to come.

There were processions, chanting, and a complex form of service. Then he was escorted to the high pulpit, wondering meanwhile why he wasn't frightened. But something sustained him.

He gazed over the large congregation, lay and clerical - all expecting some new slant on old belief. And some prepared to doze whilst well-known clichés held their sway.

"My friends," he said, "you are expecting good news of God. I come with bad news, to alert you, and to ask for a new measure of thinking from you."

Many considered that he was referring to current problems of terrorism and to his own accident. There was some increase in sympathetic attention. Something human had brushed the occasion with its wings.

"We are told," he went on, "of one Saint Paul, whose life and outlook were changed forever by a vision on the road to Damascus. I am not Saint Paul – merely an ordinary man whose vision, or lack of it, has been marked hitherto by moderation, or perhaps by mediocrity"- a slight raising of eyebrows all round. "I too have had a vision. You live here, many of you, in the midst of beautiful countryside as yet untouched by terror and war. I have to tell you that your faith is an illusion. I have seen not God, but the absence of a god. The only god, if that be the correct word, is the goodness and love in our hearts and actions. To survive, to be truly good, is to accept the new sad faith of the pessimist."

All present were now alert, amazed.

"I have seen in space the planets, the fixed stars, the nebulae, removed far from us and apparently meaningless. We are alone, on a tiny speck of matter, threatened by war, pollution, and routine unhappiness, and to comfort us we have fashioned a god to help us. Instead of leaning on this god we should shoulder our own responsibilities, put pressure on our rulers to save and make a little kinder this small place we inhabit. We can't close the churches and the temples, but we could turn them into practical vessels of love. We waste too much inward emotional energy in our religions, so called. Be realists: look around, and see the immense suffering, animal as well as human, much of it made worse by man. We are not God's finest achievements, as we have been instructed. We are worse than many animals.

"If religion is not practical it is worthless. Instead of wasting time in elaborate rituals, intellectual exercises and the wooden pursuit of old dogmas, we have to re-imagine the work of love.

"A few brave Christians, Moslems, Hindus, and those of other faiths, already work out there on the world's miserable battlefields to succour, comfort. They have the heart of the matter in them. So forget the old dogmas, out-dated, forget slavery to old texts and precepts. Listen to the great universal cry of pain. Accept the sadness and the mess of life. Only then can we begin to heal. We are not here to tell people how to live, to bully them, but to accept their diversity of need. We are not here to dictate peoples' lives, but to help and assuage, in a world where there is, it seems, no God, or where, if God exists, all-powerful, we are right to ask, 'Where is God's care for the millions, billions of suffering innocents?' God has let us down."

There were cries of "traitor", "heretic", and a few people were escorted out of the building. The preacher was led back to his stall, and the service ended as if all was normal. Then he was taken back to unrobe, in the midst of a shocked silence, and as he left the robes, said, "I shall not want them again."

In the morning the press had a fine old time. "Archbishop abandons religion. Church in disarray." "Archbishop resigns. Mentally ill after accident." "The church is in chaos. Is there a God?"

Rob suddenly knew that Emily's child was in danger.

He knew little about Dame Emily, until Mick, who was a great music-lover, brought in a friend who had attended the concert with the strange ending. As they discussed the remarkable Brahms item and the moments following, Rob became curious. He made a point of watching a TV chat show on which Dame Emily was due to appear. She had said something about telling people "more".

The TV interviewer, one of the more intelligent and sensitive of the breed, appeared to make allowance for his guest's being under some sort of stress, and much of the interview dealt at an even temperature with her early life and with her pleasure in performing works of composers with whom she felt the greatest affinity. Her list was unashamedly conventional – Beethoven, Mozart – "I love *Cosi Fan Tutte* because the great Beethoven's humour failed him and he thought the opera immoral." Although they were not at this time fashionable, she loved Tchaikovsky and Rachmaninov, and Elgar. "They gave me," she said, "so much, and I want lots of people, not merely the *cognoscenti*, to love them too. I am a popularist." There was a special tribute to Delius, "pessimistic but beautiful". And then she was asked about Brahms.

She paled slightly. "So great," she murmured. "A wonderful blend of restraint and order and good sense with passion. He can be overwhelming. At the close of Brahms 4 I had a dark vision of a tragic world almost, or completely, without hope. I should like to apologise for being overcome. Although" she hesitated – "I still believe in it."

A little later she mentioned her adopted child, and in spite of her pessimism (that word, thought Rob), her hopes for that young life.

Suddenly Rob knew. There was no point, and yet there was point, in warning her; even, as a complete stranger, acknowledging a similar vision.

He went into the garden to think. He was now living in a friendly, slightly tatty terrace house, with a long strip garden and with a tangle of shrubs at the end. "We have a family of foxes down there," Vicky had said enthusiastically.

"I must write, perhaps see her," Rob repeated to himself. And it was on the following morning that the press went wild with the Archbishop's "heresy". "Something has happened to three of us, at least. We must link up."

(8)

It was an extraordinary meeting. It had been agreed that Rob should bring Elsa, and also Mick and Vicky, who had accepted all that Rob had told them. So together they formed a sextet of enthusiastic, pessimistic, determined and friendly people.

The Archbishop, who was no more, sat in an easy chair. He was embarrassingly and informally dressed in slacks, and a pullover with a slight hint of better days. Nervous at first, after welcoming everybody, he said, "You're not getting another sermon! Briefly, three things. First, that we shouldn't be here – the Church is trying to get me out, but apparently there are legal difficulties and I can stay for a bit. Second, there's been a decent interval, and no one else seems to have had the unique vision three of us had. So it's up to us. Last, we're here to see what can and should be done, and I'm not in the chair. Enough of dictating to people. So let's discuss."

Rob was always to remember the gentle rustling of the long curtains in the window-frame whilst everyone waited in the strangest of silences. Then it was Vicky, impetuous, good-hearted, one who risked things, who got things going.

"I've been thinking all night," she said, "and perhaps I've got too many ideas, but here are some – we six, in ones or twos, could work on the project which we each feel most strongly about. And then a big meeting on radio and tele - and a statement to send out to the press, to everybody – something simple, direct." Her eyes were brimming with tears.

She had set the agenda for the day.

When they prepared to part, it was after an agreement that the emphasis of - what would be to so many people a sad and hopeless business - would be to dwell always on the need to help, reduce suffering. "In every place, in every faith, or no faith, in trade, in sport, wherever,"

The ex-bishop agreed to draft a statement for discussion and amendment. As they were leaving, he said, "No one has given me a name. Thank you for your tact! My full name is Andersley Montford Theodore, Frederick. I think you'd better call me Fred!" To cover up relieved but still embarrassed laughter, he added,

"You've already met the press outside. Be wary. Lots of people are going to hate us. I am assured that for the moment you have police protection as and when needed. I will get on to the television people."

No one had dared to speculate as to why three oddly-assorted people, with three faithful friends, had been chosen (if that was the word) to receive this burden.

"Sorry, folks, we shan't be on television. Or in any indoor venue. Apparently we are regarded by someone in power as a movement likely to encourage acts of terrorism, when our sad message is one of peace, comfort and fellowship; the only war we recognise, the war against suffering."

Fred seemed oddly facetious, as if rejecting the priestly garb had released some long-suppressed sense of fun.

"But we have a draft statement – for the world! It's short – it must be, and plainish. And before the day is out shall we allocate jobs to each one of us, as Vicky has suggested? In the hope that we can recruit other sad and disillusioned people? Oh, and shall we make plans for the only kind of meeting we can have, in the open air. I gather from a small and secretive group of clergy who are still with me, that even that has been in danger of being vetoed. We should have it soon before all our old liberties disappear in defence of freedom.

Before lunch this little group of sad loving people agreed and got things done at speeds unknown to the world's usual committees. Vicky begged to be given the animal "portfolio". "It may be the best chance I may ever have to show people how their cruelty to animals demeans our so called civilisation."

They found the necessary preface to the statement more difficult than its sequel.

"You will have heard of us. We are not cranks, as some sections of the media suggest. We three believe that we have seen the truth about our future, and yours, and three devoted friends are helping us to make this known.

"Do not dismiss us if we offend against long-held beliefs. We see that many of them are responsible for so much suffering, and our aim is not to preach to you – we have no doctrine – but to reduce suffering which is pressed upon us by the thoughtless optimism of our present values, including our obsession with money. Our world cannot be made better until we accept pessimism as a value through which we have to travel to find a greater charity. So the sadness we seek to impart to you is a means to an end, not an end in itself. It is a positive way of living to wish to reduce suffering. If we are ignore it we are guilty.

Please help us to open people's eyes."

(9)

THIS IS AN APPEAL TO YOU TO ABANDON PREJUDICES AND LIVE WITH EYES AND MINDS OPEN TO REALITY

There is no reasonable evidence for an almighty, powerful, controlling god. The world is often beautiful, but it is also a terrible mess, with one species preying upon another at every level. It is badly made: a botch. Any god-like divine spirit we feel comes from within us. If there is no overall beneficent power, there can be no ultimate authority for any religious book.

It seems to us that the world at present is not controlled by God; rather by the arms trade.

All human institutions become flawed by their very being, man having been made with so selfish a component. The law, education, politics, religion are all affected. Let your churches become channels for peace and kindness, not for dogma. Refuse to have them commandeered by the military.

The world's politicians are all more or less corrupt and incompetent. Press for <u>a new race of politicians</u>, and do not vote for them unless they have made <u>firm pledges to work for peace, disarmament and the full protection of our threatened environment</u>. At present too many leaders become indifferent autocrats, whilst our elected representatives behave like bemused sheep anxious mainly for their fodder.

Our education is geared far too much towards acquisitiveness and in the end towards war. Training for a job must be supplemented by emotional growth, awareness of personal relationships, and care for the environment, including for animal life (less destructive than our own); and it should be nourished by the open, non-dogmatic flowering of the arts (the enemies of the war party).

Accept pessimism. Be men, and be women. Stop trying not to see the horror all round us. To listen, to view the news, must convince us that progress is an illusion. The world of the missile is still the world of the cave-man, only worse.

<u>Press</u> for a body of caring people, <u>out of all nations and all faiths</u>, who will unite with one another and with all agencies working for the relief of suffering. This would be a peaceful, powerful, educational force, within which we might learn how to control events: to demand peace, disarmament, care for the planet, and ultimately a form of world citizenship. In times of darkness we must bring together all the good in the world.

The feverish optimism, pushed by much of the media, means money, power, aggression, death. If we see things with undeluded eyes then we might stop fighting and competing, and look for love and beauty in our lives. Pessimism is the start, towards undeluded, more compassionate lives, in one world; helping, comforting and supporting one another, to make our brief lives god-like <u>from within</u>.

EMILY
FREDERICK
ROBERT
WITH FRIENDS
ELSA
MICHAEL
VICTORIA

PART 3

THE APPEAL

(10)

The little group met regularly for a few days. One pleasant task was to note and plan to make use of the considerable number of supporters (some openly anxious to help, others asking for discretion to be used) – and these all mixed in with many offensive and threatening notices from the orthodox.

Amongst those expressing support, or at least sympathy, were one or two from the higher echelons of power, in the media, police, the government, the church, who "leaked" in strict confidence some disturbing news.

The centre of power (not always the obvious one) had at first, it seemed, regarded The Six, as they were now known, as harmless cranks: but they were now taken more seriously.

The message ran – that the country could not and would not accept pessimism. Business interests required a constantly hopeful looking-forward, so that people would spend more and more on material possessions. Moreover the Church had important business interests, some involving cruelty to animals, and without the message of ultimate salvation they would lose power. And the arms industry would not countenance disarmament, and ultimately world government. These measures would reduce or eliminate expenditure on wars. The churches should not get involved with these and other political issues, but should concentrate on individual goodness.

The Six were expecting responses such as these, though a little abashed by their swift arrival and (so it was reported) their ferocity.

Fred seemed to have become a new, exuberant person since throwing off his robes, not least in the face of criticism. A new emotionally open, warmer man, even a playful man, was emerging, formerly suppressed by the demands of church life. And one sudden, cheerful act touched Rob more deeply than Fred had ever consciously intended. As they were leaving one of their early planning meetings, Fred suddenly took hold of the nearest companion, who happened to be Emily, saying, "Let us all hold hands, become, as Christ said, as little children". As they formed a ring of friendship, he added, "We live in a world generally afraid of touch, except the touch of the bullet, the missile. Let's remember that in our work we are celebrating reverence for the body, including the flesh of our fellows, the animals."

As everybody held hands, something akin to an old flame which had changed his life touched Rob. In that moment of keen friendship Rob remembered Rosie; his autocratic, pushy, discouraging father, concealing deep-down real love; his rather crushed, loving mother, often sick, and later fatally so; and in the midst the rough-coated, floppy-eared dog which always welcomed him home, always loved to play, who had loved him with a complete, unquestioning love. Rosie had pined when he went away to school; had been over-joyed when he returned. When he went to university – well, Rosie, she was not there when he returned. "It was kinder to put her down. We couldn't give her your kind of attention." Later, his mother, as she lay dying, told him, "She pined so much that the vet said she could not cope without you."

Now for a moment, as The Six held hands, and then left the palace, he was not with them, as Emily had not been with her orchestra.

"Rosie, Rosie," he cried, within himself. "You showed me the full meaning of love. I could not have grown even into the man I am without you. Oh, I miss you, Rosie, Rosie, I miss you!" And then, "I hope we meet again somewhere, sometime." And then, with a rally in the soul, "Because of you I will not give up this fight. I want to make the world kinder because of you." And then they were at the gate, and going their separate ways.

(11)

Plans for the big open-air meeting were transformed by the arrival of "Stocky". In spite of high honours and a distinguished position in the Church, he now abandoned every title except his nick-name, " a residual thing" he always said, when questioned, "from my honest, happy days as a boy, before the religious got hold of me and cast a shadow over my life."

He was another one reporting a moment of vision. Though troubled by doubts for many years ("there are a lot of us like that") he had recently attended a great religious festival service of some sort. He had later played it back on television.

He saw himself, a tall, commanding presence, going through elaborate, well-rehearsed ritual, moving slowly backward and forwards and to the side, bowing, leading long prayers, intoning responses, and all accompanied by complex musical arrangements. There was from time to time a laying-on of hands as several gowned clergy ministered to the laity present. The whole made up a lengthy ceremony, after which those present were supposed to have been brought nearer to God and blessed by Him.

With a vague feeling of unease Stocky had changed TV channels casually. He was about to switch the set off when he found himself watching some sort of animal rescue in a remote part of the East Indies. In a native village, two crocodiles had been imprisoned for some years in old water-tanks, barely able to move – in one case the rusty tank was shorter than the length of the beast. With the help of local men, and at great personal risk, an animal lover and environmentalist from Stocky's home nation (he felt a sudden twinge of pride) was preparing to move them to kinder quarters – specially-prepared pools nearby. The rescuer had to tie the jaws of each animal, and after years of ill-treatment at the hands of man, as he said, they were not in good temper.

When the animals were at last in their new homes, one had to be shown how to use water, move freely.

Stocky had suddenly seen the light. This was the practical work of God, worth a whole clutch of the emotionally inward-looking church services. The "Entertainment Channel" on TV was showing an act of real worship. And when the rescuer went on to persuade villagers, against their normal thought-patterns, to release captive snakes and mammals from cages and return them to the wild, the moment of new vision was complete. This was a true laying-on of hands, Albert Schweitzer's, "reverence for life". The rest seemed tawdry.

Crocodiles were not the most lovable of animals, but they were symbols, he now knew, of the vast suffering of men and animals all over the world, all the time. He had heard something of The Six and of their compassionate pessimism, so frowned on by his Church. They were right. There were, it was true, here and there in the churches of most nations people trying to be practical, loving. But most of the time it was stultifying routine and make-believe. There was only one thing to be done with the vocation into which his good parents had placed him: chuck it.

Deciding now to be "Stocky" he contacted the former bishop and they talked about the unique vision given, as yet unexplained, to the three, and the enthusiasm of their three friends. "I want to be one," said Stocky to Fred, "and, like you, try to get the churches to see the really big things, and end all the bloody nonsense about sex, that great escape clause."

His practicality was immediate. He found a venue for a big meeting, having a useful titled university friend with a large estate. "He's Sir David, but like me he hates titles, and likes to be called David, and he's quietly with us. His place isn't too far out of town, and there's a green hill which could be a kind of pulpit."

Radio and television now ignored The Six almost completely, using a familiar technique, after the main national and international news, of filling the remaining time with trivial stuff, or squeezing embarrassing matter to the end of a slot, or out altogether. "They are increasingly worried about us," said Fred, "for they must keep people always hopeful and blind to the worst things." But the press, though satirical in reporting The Six, had reporters ready for the meeting.

Some three thousand people were expected. On the day it was more like half a million. A supporter in the transport service bravely laid on a well-advertised bus service from the town centre. "Lord D. won't want cars everywhere, and in any case might like to do a bit to encourage public transport – in line with your view of life, because cars cause so much suffering to people and to animals." Cars were kept well away from the great amphitheatre below the hill, and many family groups made a day of it, bringing children for a bus ride and a day in the country. At best it seemed like a great friendly picnic, for the day was fine and warm.

Stocky had taken over much of the back-stage arrangements, including security. "I want to do what good I can invisibly now," he said. "I've done enough in public view, elaborately gowned." He had overseen all the loudspeaker equipment, and also had an escape route ready in case of trouble, a short path into a wood where he parked the mini-bus which had brought The Six to the venue.

Safety checks on all entrants, a necessary concession made to an otherwise vaguely hostile police force, held proceedings up for a time. Meanwhile copies of the statement of aims and belief were handed to all comers. It had been agreed that Emily should speak first and that there should be limited time for questions. During the short delay, as Emily waited for a short speech of welcome from Fred, she was moved to tears by the sight of so many people, many of them children, families, young and old, at peace on a lovely day, in a still fairly decent nation; blissfully for the most part unaware of the militarism and the political fiddling and profiteering which might well bring them all to agony and utter despair; this much, with her new insights, she knew. Meanwhile the sunlit calm of a quiet autumn day, with peaceful countryside round about, and overall a pale blue sky, came to her like a tragic symbol of the happiness promised by the hoodwinkers who run the world.

Fred's short welcome speech emphasised the peaceful and unaggressive nature of all the little group on the platform stood for. "We are not here," he was anxious to assure his audience, "to put any kind of pressure on you. We just ask you to think new things, and perhaps consider stopping doing certain things which cause suffering. Our vision of the world is one in which there is more peace because there is more kindness. I welcome you all and wish to introduce Dame Emily."

It was a good move to open with a speech from a woman and from an artist, breathing the emotional insight and a capacity to see beyond principles and precepts denied to so many men.

"Dear friends," she said, "may I add to Fred's welcome, and thank you for coming. I am not going to talk for long – none of us will – for we want you to enjoy this lovely day out.

"I want to say, straight away, that – in spite of some absurd rumours – we are not terrorists! Rather we are the opposite to terrorists, for terrorists cause suffering, and we want, with your valued help, to try to reduce suffering, some of which we are not encouraged to see. For some reason, one or two of us have been led to see, and feel, the sadness of this world in a special way, and we think we might join hands with some of you kind people to begin to ease the world's sadness. I say begin because the problem, globally, is so immense, and indeed so many people's work depends on pain, that to try too hard will overwhelm and dishearten us. But we can begin to chip away at the pain, and I'm going to suggest ways of doing that about which we can press governments and other interests here and now, in ways which don't imperil the livelihoods of the people who cause pain.

"I lie awake at night, dear friends, thinking of the very cruel and unnecessary killing of whales. These are intelligent and sociable animals like us: at any moment of any day someone is harpooning and dragging these sensitive creatures on board ship to keep up a "quota". And dolphins and albatrosses are captured and killed by cruel fishing lines.

"Some zoos, not all, and some circuses, cause distress to animals, and the unnatural life they may have to lead can be changed if you stop supporting such activities. And is it necessary to make money by importing and selling for the pet trade creatures which should be in the wild with others, not brought overseas under cruel conditions and often, when here, inhumanly kept in captivity, stuck perhaps in cages or in small glass tanks? Again you can help, by pressing for an end to the kind of pet shop trade which causes distress to animals. Because we are kind, and aware of suffering, we can protest about the cruel killing of baby seals, and about the fur trade generally. In these and in other ways you can assist by writing, or by refusing "cruel" goods.

"My colleagues will be speaking about two obvious issues - pollution and war. I'll leave these great matters to them. No less controversial are two other matters.

"So I'll end my list of horrors with those two items. We just don't think enough about them, and we should be encouraged so to do.

"The first is transport. So many deaths, serious injuries and bereavements, are due to road transport. We should be building fewer roads and putting money into safer ways of travel. I am thinking of our trains, which are having a bit of a revival, but not enough, and need to be returned to the comprehensive coverage of the whole country which they once had, and made comfortable, convenient and safe, to the highest standards. Otherwise buses, and especially trams, should be the norm in our cities, where at present cars clog up and pollute our streets in huge numbers.

"My last point is even more controversial, but I must make it, for the sake of kindness. There are too many people in the world. Global resources are not endless, and too much land is being taken for building. That land is needed for agriculture, and the country for our emotional needs, and for animals, who are being driven out of their traditional territories, sometimes taking revenge on the usurping human race. Endless population growth is going to cause wars, pestilence, famine and drought. Those who oppose contraception are therefore causing suffering, but they will not accept the consequences. It is wrong to expect too much from people and then ignore the population growth which will follow.

"I say all these things not for the sake of confronting anybody, but for the sake of kindness. I think especially of the children who are going to inherit the sorry mess we are making of our poor Earth at present. Our little group feels that we live in a difficult world, in which suffering is continuous and in many cases unnecessary. Please help us to challenge the insensitive optimism of our rulers, in many lands. If they were kinder, there would not only be less suffering, but the world would also be a more sensible, more rational place. They should not be ruled by profit or desire for power, or prestige, but by loving imagination and care. Please help us to help them towards a union of love with good sense.

Thank you."

Emily's speech, with its moderation, its very human touches, and her friendly, quiet tone, brought a long round of applause, with only the odd boo, the odd slow hand-clap, from disaffected people here and there.

There was a short break before half a dozen or so folk were invited to provide comments and questions.

Their comments were for the most part reasonable and politely put. Several people backed up all Emily had said, adding in several cases their own worries about the environment. Another said that God was the only answer we needed. Another had to be checked after speaking at length about the production of margarine, and yet another tried to drum up support for a tiny party of his own called The Apostles of Light. On the whole it was all good-tempered.

Rob was distinctly worried in spite of the feeling that all so far had gone well. He had not forgotten his prophetic insight about Emily and her child. There was a second worry: Vicky. She was anxious to speak next. Of those who had not yet spoken, Stocky apart, none called themselves eloquent or were used to making a public address, except Vicky. Her lively, enthusiastic manner seemed likely to hold an audience. But Rob had prescience that for all her tremendous goodness and charity of heart, she might go over the top. She always spoke what was in her heart, and sometimes thought afterwards.

As she rose to speak, Fred, with, it seemed, similar worries, leant over and whispered, "Go easy. Remember that we're just at the beginning. We'll get on to the big things if we wait and if we're lucky."

If anyone was likely to rouse up opposition, it would be Vicky, but this might have been worth the risk if her emotional power could win over so many. Rob noticed a group of sullen, blank-looking men near the stage, waiting, it seemed, for the next round of questioning.

She began well with details of her work with deprived children in Africa, and went on to talk about her love for ill-treated and captive animals out there. Her eyes were moist. "I feel that animals are closer to us than we think, and feel so much as we do. Our kindness to them will spill over into kindness to our own kind." She spoke about the benefits of having a pet, especially for children. She recalled Christ's blessing of little children, and for a moment dwelt on the tenderness and sensitivity of much of the gospel story. Then she said, as if to follow on was natural, "That's why I hate to think of poor little calves, separated from their mothers almost at birth, and sent away by road and ship crated for the veal trade."

This was dodgy. They all agreed with her, as did many members, probably, of the audience, but had agreed for the moment to avoid direct comment on any trade which furnished a livelihood, for the moment at least. There were cries from a segment of the crowd which seemed pretty solid, "Leave the meat trade alone!"

"I'm sorry!" she added, beginning now to weep, "But when I see the carcasses hanging up in the butcher's I think of how they deserved better, and what they have gone through." A chorus of dissent and resentment from the meat traders was growing into a steady growl. "I don't want to upset you," Vicky cried, above an increasing uproar, "but try to imagine the feelings of the lamb taken from the ewe, and how the mother must feel."

Rob and Fred were urgently trying to stop her. "Leave this for the moment."

Vicky made a separate throw, which was again ill-judged at the time. "May I appeal to the churches," she cried, "for their help in putting forward a gospel of love?"

It was becoming clear that even Stocky had underestimated the presence of interested groups with protests to make. In another part of the grounds a group rose as one and a banner was unfurled, "Don't deny God!", and another, "God will exact revenge upon sinners." This group began to push its way forward, singing a hymn. Then the meat people also began to push towards the centre, shouting. At the back a few people, particularly those with children, were beginning to leave.

"May I beg you all," Fred pleaded, "to allow this meeting to continue in a peaceful way? There will be an opportunity for people to make their points." Stocky was making calls to his own security personnel and to the bus people. For a moment it seemed that Fred's calming voice had worked, until a tall man with a megaphone rose from the middle of the crowd. "If you've all read the silly blurb they've given out, you'll know that this lot want to give up our defensive weapons and disarm the nation. They are dangerous and foolish. Don't listen any more."

At this point some of the men who had been seen crowding round the base of the speakers' platform began to force their way towards The Six. At once Stocky prepared to get his friends away through the escape route at the back and into the mini-bus. "Quickly, to Dame Emily's house." But Fred would not move, and as soon as the others had left, including a weeping Vicky, guilt-ridden and forlorn, he was joined by Stocky, who was in time to see one of the intruders seize Fred, who was still appealing for order, and throw him over the grassy bank on which they stood. The effect of the fall might not have been critical on that soft earth, but it became the signal for a general wave of mass madness in which all protestors appeared for the moment to act as one.

Before Stocky could reach Fred, two or three evil-looking men, unnoticed before, began to beat the fallen man with sticks, which should never have been allowed in. Someone else, a compassionate soul, was observed bending over Fred as the men with staves disappeared into the crowd. Stocky, noticing that Fred had some assistance, and not realising the seriousness of the attack, gave priority to the getting of families, and children especially, out of the grounds. He strode through the middle ground, the religious zealots on the one hand and traders on the other seeming to give ground as he appealed for safety for the innocent and uninvolved. His authority worked: one or two security personnel caught up with him. Amazingly everyone found their way out with little more than a few cuts and bruises, though many were terrified and in tears. The aggressors, their work done, melted away. Only then did Stocky return towards the platform. A doctor was bending over Fred, who was dead.

No one had been found to apprehend or even provide names of the men who had broken his skull and left him bleeding.

(12)

The blows of another kind which now fell upon the other members of The Six were enough to persuade them to give up hope, be warned by a cruel providence, a cruel fate. There was Vicky to comfort, and her remorse was devastating to her and to her friends. There was the death of the man who, without meaning to, had led and inspired the others, as well as befriending them. But when the little party reached Emily's house, the third blow fell. Her child had been taken from the garden whilst her minder had been briefly occupied with a phone call.

Unafraid of the physical as they were, there was a great deal of mutual comfort to be given, hands touching, arms round shoulders. Vicky was able to forget to some extent her own sense of failure whilst holding in her arms the sorrowing and shocked mother.

It was assumed that the kidnapping was part of a reaction to The Six, and like Vicky, Emily was wondering whether her speech, though so very different, as well as so much of her earlier support for the group, had contributed to death and loss. Stocky, the as yet newish friend, stood a little apart, in the sunset twilight of that afternoon.

Fred, whilst disclaiming the position, had always been the unacknowledged leader. Now, with Emily *hors de combat* for the moment, Rob, as the last member of the original three, attended at once to security. Police were supposed to be guarding Emily's house, but he organised a more discreet venture of his own, with the help and advice of Sir David, who had resolutely refused help in the clearing up of the mess left after the débâcle of the big meeting. Perhaps they were all now at risk at a new level. And of course, readily pursued enquiries about the missing child.

Everybody stayed together overnight.

They were then visited by the police investigating Fred's murder. It became clear that four had left in the minibus before the fracas around the platform had peaked, whilst Stocky was trying to get people to safety, some distance away. Only Fred would have known his attackers well. But some evidence concerning men seen near the platform before the assault was noted. There was still a marked dearth of response to appeals for information from the audience, including the church group and the butchery people. No one had seen the kidnapping of Emily's child.

No one felt able to do much until after Fred's funeral, which was held up whilst enquiries were completed. When it did come, the farewell to the former archbishop who had seen a new sort of faith was a sparse affair. Held in the local crematorium, with no clergy officiating, the tiny congregation included the remaining five plus a distant cousin of Fred's – a shy, elderly lady who declined all hospitality and disappeared as soon as the ceremony ended: plus a few brave clergy, old colleagues of Fred's. These last were courageously risking official disapproval, and even physical danger. For though held back by a police cordon, a far larger congregation waited outside, holding banners - "Those who deny life will never attain eternal life," "Death to the traitor." Inside Stocky spoke briefly about faithfulness to vision, but in a sense which the mob outside would not have recognised.

The small meal which followed was unlike the normal sad but affable gathering after a death. Emily and Vicky were again in tears. Police came once or twice, but there was no news of Fred's murderers or of Emily's child. One or two of the private investigators reported quietly to Emily. A car had been seen near the house at the time of the abduction. There was a description of sorts, but no registration number.

In the air, as they all knew, was the unanswered question – Shall we go on? Are we meant to go on? Whilst they were still quietly joined in fellowship they had a visit from the Deputy Chief Constable. He brought the news that The Six were henceforth forbidden to address any meeting of more than fifteen persons. Someone "higher up" had concluded that they had been a threat to public order. One or two present detected a hint of a sympathetic and ironic movement of the official's face as he delivered the news.

It was Elsa who provided a breakthrough. For a moment the sad, shadowed group had dispersed. Mick and Vicky had gone into the garden, where for the moment Emily could not bear to set foot – she had gone to her room for a moment of private grief. It was always easy to "forget" Elsa, with her slight figure and her quiet dark beauty, especially in the presence of Vicky, with her flamboyant romantic clothing and loveliness, though just now without *joie de vivre*. Now Elsa approached her lover, and their new friend, Stocky.

She went and stood between them, an arm round Rob, her free hand clasping Stocky's. Both seemed ready to hear from the most retiring, the quietest member of The Six.

"I think," she said, "that we should hold on just now to the friendship and love we have enjoyed as a group. That may have a lot of meaning, though I don't think we should be looking for meaning just now. I think it would help if we all remembered the good things from the past, including from our childhoods, even if there have been bad things there amongst the good. We all need ballast just now, to remember who we are.

"And then about the future. As you all know, I have rejected religion as we know it. I realise now that any sort of dogma, any fixed creed, prevents full understanding of life; and our group, as Rob has shown me, is about trying to bring people to a full understanding. But the Bible, as I remember from my church days, says some lovely things about love and forgiveness and the rejecting of violence, just as the sacred books of other religions do too. And I did wonder whether our answer to ourselves, now, would be to go out in ones and twos, like Christ's disciples. We can't hold big meetings. But we can talk to people. After all, we have, unlike Christ's disciples, no dogma, no faith to push, except that people should be made more aware, not be taken in by the heartless optimism of our society."

Stocky and Rob listened to the quiet woman's words with a degree of wonder. Rob already knew the silent treasures of her being, her transformation of a wretched youth, and her past mistakes, into a great positive, a capacity for healing. Stocky had hitherto under-estimated her.

He broke the silence. "You have shown us the way," he said, the more tightly grasping her hand. "So much of the Bible, like other books from other faiths, is contradictory, out of touch with real life today, and sometimes so insensitive to the real needs of people. But you have shown us how not to throw the baby out with the bath-water. We must be grateful."

And so it was agreed. Why did everything work so smoothly with so little argument, even with a certain joy? In the work they had to do they had no ambition, only awareness that the dreadful testosterone-driven thing, the evolutionary fault, the man thing, which has raised great cities, fought so many battles, invented so much that is brilliantly clever, now for lack of the other part of life threatens to extend suffering and then destroy the world. They valued that instinctive, non-dogmatic mode of life which was discovered more often in women – the desire to protect and cherish life, to be personal, not general. By that same token as they talked about their past lives it became clear that Stocky was gay, as they all suspected. There was no barrier to be raised. The dogmas of social or religious convention were alien to the central message of love.

Stocky was wanting, though not pressing it too hard, to take on the church "portfolio": to try again to get the clergy to feel, tackle the big things, put love in place of harsh judgement. Rob took the education file, finding in it, as he did, so much of the bad and the worst things of his own life. Vicky naturally took on the animal brief. Nick wished to be with her in this, but had a further interest in the most difficult and complex task – of tackling the political scene. Emily, with connections to the higher life of society, felt that she might find a few strings to pull. She was closer than ever before to William Blake, to the union of art with political life: that, far from art's being in a world of its own it had something to say about society and how to live: and had connections, as Blake had discovered, with religion, and not merely in terms of sacred words and beliefs, being beyond belief. She also wished passionately to put forward the truth that (military music apart) music and the liberal arts in general, were more deeply opposed to war than any other branch of knowledge, and that it was right and proper for women to put that case. Mick as a brave, experimental dramatist was anxious to help.

There were practical considerations. It was agreed that Rob and Elsa would stay at Emily's place. "Your company will be so precious to me just now," she said. Vicky and Mick were still living at their old house. Stocky, determined to remain independent, at last found a guest house that would take him in – after many refusals, not all polite. Sir David was secretly helping to fund them all, and a further anonymous donor was contributing generously. In the end they would have to find work again. But for the moment they could manage.

All things work together for good for those who have followed love and given up power. They would meet regularly at Emily's, hoping to ease a little the special tension she was under. No one was in charge. They had no leader. "Leaders are almost always bad," said Stocky.

(13)

Vicky, though with less reason than Emily to be depressed and disturbed, was advised to take a short holiday with her partner. Her lively imagination, with her more than with most, kept her, more often than was useful, painfully alert to the multitude of pains and sorrows which man inflicts on animals, year after year. Every news item in the press or on the radio about the needless suffering of animals left her so saddened as to have less energy for the work of kindness. It was the thoughtlessness, so much as the deliberate savagery: the "jolly hunting-trips", on land, in the air and in the world's waters.

Mick tried to get her to dwell for the minute on the pleasant, gently undulating country in which a friend had let them have a cottage for a couple of weeks.

They decided to forget their work in the world, if they could, and climb a sizeable hill some three miles distant, take a picnic, and be as children again.

They set off towards the end of the village street where a pleasant footpath struck off across wheat fields. As they passed the last village dwelling, Vicky detected a faint mewing. She stopped, as she always did when she met a cat, to give it a brief pat and a stroke: but a closer look revealed a very thin and bedraggled long-haired ginger cat, once possibly an expensive and rather special pet for someone. Its lovely coat was tangled up and filthy, and its emaciated condition suggested a lost and abandoned creature.

When she picked it up it seemed almost weightless. Unwilling to leave it as it was, she suggested that Mick should go on ahead and take extra time to linger over wild flowers, one of his special interests; a healthful change from the stress of the theatre. Left alone, Vicky made enquiries: no one appeared to own the cat. She begged one elderly lady, who looked with concern at the filthy and forlorn creature, for the use of a phone to get help from an animal rescue service. "Don't put it in my house", said the old lady, "but you could leave it in my shed until they come for it." Vicky begged for urgent help from an over-worked and under-resourced charity, and was promised rescue within the half an hour. After buying some pet cat food from the village shop, and pressing a banknote into the frightened lady's hand, she set off again, arranging to call on her way back. The cat seemed, as she left, too weak to eat, and she feared for it. Lost, or abandoned, she wondered, the property of an elderly person deceased?

Still anxious, but knowing that she had done her best for a suffering creature, she pressed ahead along the footpath. She could see Mick far ahead, until his form disappeared over a ridge. The terrain gradually changed from fields into scattered woodland and then into moorland, as they climbed. Over to the left, some way off, Vicky noticed a line of grouse butts. Can one never get away from reminders of man's inhumanity to animals, she wondered? But there was no sound of shooting. She went on, climbing, trying to set aside an all-pervasive darkness, until she crested another slope and saw the immensity of the moor, the shooting butts; and, nearer, Mick, surrounded by a threatening group of three or four men in outdoor clothing, one of whom appeared ready to strike him, but was held back by another.

"Leave him alone," Vicky screamed, rushing towards the threatening group. "He is my love. Leave him. He has done nothing but good here, or in the world."

One of the men eyed Vicky up and down. "Well, well, well, this is a bonus!" He made as if to approach her. "Leave her," cried Mick. "Tell me what you want, the lot of you, and let us go."

"We know who you are," another man said. "We've seen the newspapers. We knew you were on our path, and stopped shooting. But we'll be at it again in a moment, and by that time you'll be gone!"

Mick thought, "How do they know so much about us?" Vicky was thinking of the lady with the telephone.

She was trembling with fear, but Mick had to say it. "You breed birds trustingly, and then scare them so that they fly in fear and then you shoot them down. You are concealed: they are not. Do you consider this sport? And have you looked at the beauty of one of the bird's body, the delicacy of its feathers, and how ugly it is fallen and bloody and dying?"

"Shut up!" said one man, moving closer to Mick, even raising his gun. The one who had first spoken turned towards Vicky and began to tug at her skirt. "Leave it," commanded another, "and you two get off and don't come back." "How ugly are the faces of these men," murmured Mick. "What was that?" someone queried. "We're going," said Vicky, "but you should all be ashamed".

"Have we done any good?" It was the shared thought as they turned back disconsolately.

And they were now being watched, all the time. Their democratic nation had been edging towards a form of despotism for some time.

When they reached the village they enquired about the cat. "A man came, but it had already died. He said it must have been on the run for weeks, but nobody had ever taken it in."

"What makes men like that?" Vicky whispered. A little calmer, Mick replied, "A lot of it is tradition. It's always been done. We are fighting not merely evil acts, but barriers, clichés, in the mind of man."

"I want to go back," Vicky said, "to where there are kind people who have not been afraid to think new things." Mick urged another rather more peaceful day in the country.

But even this was to be altered. On their next morning they heard the horns of the huntsmen, and within the hour hounds and men on horses were moving through the village, watched by housewives in pinafores and children waiting for their school bus, rather as villagers had done during centuries of tradition. "Don't go!" Vicky implored her lover. "You're needed by Emily and the others and me!" "I'll be careful," he replied, "but before we leave this beautiful and benighted place, we must make our point."

At first, to Vicky's guilt-ridden relief, the hunt disappeared noisily into a distant wood. There are times when the spent heart cannot take any more of the world's suffering, and Vicky was near that point. Then the hunt returned at speed across fields behind the village and came to a stop on the crest of a distant hillock.

As if with one mind Vicky and Mick ran forward, finding themselves within a minute or two faced with a small stream. They were in a small but lovely valley. The clear and peaceful stream was alive with fish, mostly small, but often exquisitely marked. They wished to stay for a moment. The sound of the hunt was hushed. Then the lovers waded across, taking care to cause little disturbance to the beautiful and innocent life of the water. As they mounted the hillock a large man saw them and consulted with another rider. Moving down fast towards them, even aggressively, he said, "This is private land. Please leave."

"It can't be trespassing to try to save life," said Mick meekly.

The man's eyes widened. "I know now who you are. You hate our sport, because it's sport. Get out!" He raised his whip.

"I'd like to know," said Mick, again quietly. "what is going on at the top of the hill" The large man relaxed a little; proud of his position "We've had a good morning. We've killed a large she-fox, and just now we're dealing with her cubs."

"What do you mean, dealing with the cubs?"

"They will be dug out and given to the dogs. Less cruel than leaving them to starve after the bitch has been destroyed."

A number of riders had now come down, forming a rough semicircle round Mick and Vicky. "I'd just like to ask," said Mick, struggling to keep his voice and his rage down, "how it can be a sport when a dozen or more strong men and women on strong horses can chase one small terrified animal. When two teams play soccer in equal numbers it's a fair sport. This is so unfair as to be almost a massacre. How can it be sportsmanlike, in the good old-fashioned sense?"

One of the huntsmen moved his horse forward. "Leave it," said a voice on one side. This was from the leader of the hunt. Mick noted that in any bad situation there were usually one or two, more decent than the rest, as there had been with the grouse-shooters when Vicky had been in danger. But Vicky was *in extremis* again. She said, "What bad faces! That beautiful animal you have killed was more beautiful to behold than you lot."

There was a movement of anger towards the two. The leader again asked for restraint, but not before one horse had knocked Mick down as the rider's whip lashed his shoulders. The sight of the motionless body, and of a woman turning the body over with bitter weeping, was the spur for an ordered withdrawal. The leader called for help on his mobile, then turned angrily to Vicky. "You've brought this on yourselves, silly bastards!"

Mick was moaning a little. Vicky lay above him, cradling him.

Twenty minutes later, Mick was being carried to an ambulance. The van's door remained open while some sort of first aid was administered. Vicky became aware of one rider, a young girl, who had separated herself from the main body of the hunt. She was slim, pale and fair. Vicky left her lover to paramedics for a moment, and, red-eyed, sensed there was something more to be said.

"I'm sorry," said the pale girl. "I'm the daughter of one of the huntsmen. Father persuaded me to come; and you're right. It's a cruel business. But don't expect that you'll get any sympathy, even justice, if it comes to the courts. They will all close ranks round here. You've upset a tradition. And the local magistrate was riding here today." The girl turned to the ambulance. "Will he be all right?" she asked. To Vicky's surprise the young rider was now in tears herself. "Do you know what one of that lot -" she motioned towards the departing huntsmen - "said about you? He said, 'Tell that girl to leave our country and its habits alone, and go back to teach the niggers in Africa.' I felt so ashamed. Even here we don't usually insult men and women, perhaps better than us, with that terrible word. I am so ashamed. That remark made me see the light." She turned, "I am apologising to your man," she said. "I am now going to be different." She turned and rode off quickly.

Mick had some form of concussion and possibly an injury to the brain. Further tests were going to be necessary.

A kindly nurse put Vicky up for the night. Was someone telling them to stop? Had they achieved nothing?

After one of Vicky's daily visits to the hospital where Mick was lying, intermittently conscious, Rob said, "You know, it all falls into one area of discourse - education." He was trying to distract her, be general, to mitigate the new stresses she was under.

"Tell me more." she said gently.

He went on, "Really, one feels sorry for these people who have hurt you so badly." Before she could protest he went on, "Because they are emotional cripples. They believe that they have been educated, but either for genetic reasons, or because of a bad childhood, or a sterile schooling, they have never felt the stirrings of imagination. So they cannot imagine the feelings of animals they torture. Their upbringing has left little time for the cultivation of the emotions. You, my love, have been the victim of emotional cripples, clever, efficient, well-respected, and spiritually undeveloped.

"These people cannot change. But you have seen one young person change. You have helped her to grow."

He went on; with his arm round Vicky, "Your portfolio leads on to mine. Your remit is mine. If there is a Kingdom of heaven, the key to it is imaginative love. That is where goodness begins.

The world is dying for lack of it."

(14)

In many societies, leagues, parties, there exists a moderate to radical campaign group, which exists to keep alive the broken promises of its leaders.

This is true of more than one elected government, when an essential life-giving message, on whose merits people have been elected, has been lost amid compromise, jockeying for power, time-serving, and pressure from other nations. So it was with the education world, whose central body The Six could not address, but whose most honourable and uncorrupted group, a small one, met separately to try to keep the pure flame alive.

This splinter group was meeting in a small room at the side of the main hall during a major conference. Someone present had read The Six's set of principles and had noted the comments on education which had chimed in with much of the group's thinking. Rob's booking as a speaker had been criticised by the conference's central committee, but the strong-minded lady chairperson of the "awkward squad", as they were sometimes called, had got her way.

"I have a daughter of secondary school age," she said, as, after welcoming colleagues and their guest speaker, she sought to open up discussion. "She is a bright girl, but is so miserable at school because it has been turned into a business college and its god is the computer. I acknowledge, I emphasise this, that some pupils have to be prepared for jobs in business, but my girl who loves music and drama and the dance and writes poetry, feels that the place which she once loved has lost its soul.

"We'd like your views, too, on another sort of school or college, where everything is served up in bits, hundreds of units to collect over the years, some on subjects totally unrelated to the others. At the end you're in the life-boat for qualifications and a job if you've collected the requisite number of passes. You don't remember most of them, or the relevance of anything studied.

"And there's another type of school which is worrying so many of us. These are encouraged to go private, or partly so, and be directed by a board made up of people who may stand for business interests, or for a set faith or moral dogma, which is not necessarily appropriate for all pupils, or fit well into a broad, tolerant, and open-minded view of the world, which is surely one great aim of education.

"We feel that our good friends in the big meeting upstairs, many of them valued colleagues, are less worried than they should be about trends like these. At the moment they are discussing contracts and salaries.

"Your group of Six appears to be with us in our worries. May we share your concerns, and possibilities for action?"

At that moment Rob, who had been keenly listening, became aware of a shock which was too diffuse to be felt as before. Only later did he realise that it had happened again, perhaps with less apocalyptic force. Once he had seen the dark past and the awesome future. Now he was elsewhere.

The scene was irrelevant, and yet so relevant. It was the recent past, and he was a boy again. He was still attending the village school, although his father didn't like the mixing with "the village people". But father was often away at this time on military business, and his mother was quietly pleased that Rob got on so well with Jasper. Jasper! How long was it since Rob had thought of him - about his own age, his best pal at school. One didn't cry in a sort of dream, and yet he was gently crying to remember the walks with Jasper and a younger Rosie: picnicking in the woods, playing football with Jasper and Rosie: and comfortable, homely teas at Jasper's house.

Jasper's father had left his wife and child some years before, and the boy might have been left permanently disturbed. But the steady love of his mother, his open friendship with other children within a secure village community, and the support of the village school, saved him, and he seemed to move towards adulthood unblemished.

The school! This had been the key which had brought back the vision. There were only two teachers, the Head, who was going on in years, and an enthusiastic young woman who taught the little ones and was keen to open up the hearts and minds of her charges to the full richness of the natural world around them. In those days there was little outside interference in the running of the school. The vicar popped in from time to time, and an occasional inspector was given tea and biscuits, and remarked on the friendliness and relaxed order of the place. The skeletal discipline – no bullying, no rudeness to staff or to one another – these and other quietly understood traditions kept the school happy, under the aegis of a Head who was more like a father to his pupils than a remote despot.

It was not heaven: some of the village children were dirty. A nurse came sometimes to check and occasionally get help for very neglected children, and sometimes had to cope with head-lice. But the memories were mostly of nature walks with the young assistant teacher, the identifying of wild flowers, the bird-watching, and the fun of Christmas celebrations. Like a good family, the school held children together, combining attention to the three R's, in the early part of the school day, with a developing sense of the wonder of the world around them. Rob could remember the shaming, approved of by almost all fellow-pupils, of a boy who had rifled and destroyed a bird's nest.

The class thing, he remembered, was not entirely absent. He recalled with slight embarrassment his mother's saying, "Your friend Jasper must come to your birthday tea. Let's ring his mother up." Rob had had to tell his mother that there was no telephone at Jasper's house.

What had happened? Why was society now so violent, inside school as well as outside? At the tough boarding school to which his father at last sent him, where were the child-centred diaries of achievement and enthusiasm, the love of learning, the sense of belonging to one another? Now there was the work, the graphs, the weekly attainment tests, the overpowering sense of guilt, the loneliness; but sometimes the human smile of one of the staff who was "different". One such said on the side to his class, "It's a lousy system lads, all the testing and pressure and exams, but we've got to go through with it, and then towards the end of term we can enjoy ourselves a little."

There they were all boys. He missed one or two of the village girls who were friendly and jolly. But he missed Jasper and he missed Rosie; and it was a great excess of grief for Rosie which brought him back where he was, to here and now; Rosie who met him from afternoon school with his mother, ran with him through the woods and meadows, and pined for him when he was sent away. He was suddenly aware of a number of those present looking curiously at him, in the small rather plain room at the conference centre.

"I'm sorry," he stammered. It appeared that time had been "absent" for a few seconds only.

Still half in another world, Rob remembered his brief to demonstrate that so much was wrong, that there was a neglected dimension about education. The big meeting in the main room was where discussion was needed. But with the concerned minority he described education good and bad, the village school, the forcing-house of later years, and the forces behind the forcing-houses, the pressures of industry, and perhaps of war. He pleaded for widespread teaching of parenthood, so that new generations would have known love, peace of mind and tolerance. It was now known that kids from a tough, pressurised home, or no home, grew up the more inclined to extremism, to think generally, not about individuals, to be anxious and excessive in thought and action.

They discussed the schools under the aegis of private bodies, industrial, religious. It was all wrong: their guild of teachers, he insisted, should resist it.

Once you started to inculcate dogma you cut off a full understanding of the world, you necessarily limit that understanding. Schools should remain in the care of local people, All options, all faiths, should be presented.

We wish, Rob concluded, to end war and crime. How many of the criminals in disguise who encourage war, who love nations and empires more than people, how many of these have been crippled emotionally by bad parent-craft or none?

At the close he was warmly applauded. The time-slip into the vision had given his thinking and speaking an extra edge. He left feeling that something had been accomplished.

He moved to catch his bus. On the far side of the road a large car began to follow him, and then drew level. His euphoria began to ebb away: I am going to be kidnapped, or shot, he decided. He quickened his pace towards the main street, without shaking off the pursuers.

A voice, not unkind, said, "Rob, I wish to speak with you."

"It's a trap," he considered, and tried once more to outstrip the car. Then the voice said, "Rob, we know you. Please stop."

Something in the inflexion of the voice, still with a country burr, made Rob stop, look into the car.

There was someone else in the back, but the speaker was looking at Rob full in the face from the driver's seat. He was a man of about Rob's age. Clean-shaven, neat, in a dark suit.

A movement of the face muscles, a humorous twitch around the eyes, but above all the kindness which obstinately lingered through the official voice, brought Rob to a stop.

"It isn't. It can't be. How can it be? Are you Jasper?"

"Hello, old friend."

There was a slight movement at the back of the car.

"How can you be here, after all these years? Here, today?"

Rob made a move towards his old friend, perhaps to grasp the hand, but Jasper made no complementary move.

"This conversation is strictly illegal. My associate here has promised to keep his counsel."

"How did you find me? I thought you went to work on the railway."

"I did, and then I joined the railway police. Then they started closing the railways, and I took a job in security. I can't tell you more. We know a great deal. You were known to be speaking here today. Rob, it's no use."

"No use?"

"I've come, illegally, to warn you. Stop all your campaigning, the lot of you, and, if you can, get out of the country. We are supposed to be one of the best democracies, but because of the fear of terrorism, but also because you and your friends threaten the whole world they represent, they will get you in the end. Special orders to imprison you, or - like Dame Emily's child."

"Was the…?"

"I can't say. The whole place is bugged. All your significant movements are known."

"But the terrorism threat seems less just now."

"It's so much more than that. You are a threat to the whole consumer society. People must think that life is always going to be happier if they buy more. They aren't. And war. The state has to keep threatening wars all the time to please the military-industry people, who have the final absolute power over all of us. You want peace. But it's no good, ever."

Something about the difference between the dark, almost monotonous speech and the happy village boy he had known, overtook Rob, and he cried, "Leave it all, Jasper! Come over and join us. I remember your good mother – tell me about her. And do you remember Rosie? There have been good times. You've proved our point. Life is terrible. Let's change it, or get out."

"I can't leave," said Jasper. "I have signed up. And mother died two years ago." There was a pause. "She always liked you." With a new emphasis he suddenly almost cried, in a different, scary voice. "I have to do my work. I have a family to look after. But I will tell you that the things I know about government are so terrible that I believe that to run a decent state brothel would be more honourable, less deceitful than the running of the country. Lies, lies, lies. And all the tricks of the orator cannot disguise them." His voice dropped a little "A few try for better things."

Rob heard another slight movement in the back of the car. "I must go," Jasper said. "I have said forbidden things. Remember, dear old friend, there's no real hope for better things. I fear for you. Get out. Lie low, or get abroad."

The car leapt forward and he was gone. It all felt like a dream, or rather a nightmare.

For a moment Rob savoured again the grim irony. His old friend had proved his own point, his own pessimism.

(15)

Pearson, editor of "The Shield", was gazing over the withered lawn which extended to the ring of small trees which marked the boundary of his garden. He had breakfasted well, and was waiting to take his two grandchildren for a walk before the heat became too intense. The country home, well-loved, which he saw too little of because of his work in the capital, was quiet and relaxing: but his wife had half joked with him about the "new look" on his face. He was a concerned man, and the editor-in-chief of one of the more liberal dailies. He was usually cheerful and forward-looking.

The excited children arrived, dressed for the weather, with buckets and fishing-nets, and instructions to put any small fish caught into their garden pond. They passed out of the garden and along a path over parched fields, and crossed the bed of a brook, now dry.

Ahead was a little hill and a jolly race over it to be first at the river.

The children stood and looked doubtfully at the valley.

Hardly moving, the stream now seemed to be made up of isolated pools, with a thin trickle in the middle showing the once true path of the river. The tiny waterfall just above which the children had always loved and played around was no longer there.

With the optimism of youth the children began to build dykes and deeper pools here and there, and found small fish trapped; rescued them to take home. Less hopeful was the plight of other fish gasping for breath, and some still larger fish, lifeless, in the remains of the natural environment which had been their home.

It was becoming hotter under the few scant trees bordering the river, and with the prospect of elevenses the family party set off for home. Over the big field behind the garden, the sun, once a giver of life celebrated by poets down the ages, was now more like a harsh, brazen malevolence, made worse by the film of pale heat mist behind which its intensified power lay. With care the family party carried home the small collection of rescued fish, taking turns not to spill the pail, into the garden and straight to the pool, itself lower than it should have been. "Grandpa, we mustn't put too much cold tap-water in at any one time. A sudden drop in temperature will hurt the fish." Someone had been teaching them the right kind of science, the human kind, their grandfather considered, as he went to get the garden hose. The children were feeding the fish now, enjoying their new pets, which rose eagerly to the surface as if starving, which they probably were.

Reminding the children not to stay too long in the sun, Charles Pearson went back to the armchair which had furnished the setting for his earlier morning meditation. His wife brought coffee, and stood close to him. "Is it the news, my love? In your line of country you must be well used to it, and yet..."

"It does seem worse than ever," he replied, taking her hand. "We call ourselves 'the international community' and civilised. Give us a chance and we start fighting with stone-age savagery. Men in expensive suits killing children, saying sorry, but they don't really care." He paused. "Let's be happy here today."

He took her hand and they were silent for a moment. The burning heat was uncomfortable even with the French windows open. The family cat had sensibly retired to a cool hidey-hole under the stairs, but the old Labrador crept in and went to sleep at their feet. Their younger daughter, Sophie, heavily pregnant, joined them from the room where she had been resting. The heat was bad for her too. Pearson looked at her with affection, but today with new thoughtfulness. He could hear her first two children playing upstairs, perhaps on a computer or with a card game or painting. Everything seemed, weather apart, well-ordered, sensible and with love. He said, "Will you excuse me just for a moment or two? I want to write a letter."

(16)

In the study he looked again at the previous Sunday's "Shield". The reporting had, he still felt, been properly sympathetic, and the incident was forcing a shift in public opinion about The Six. A dead child found in a suburban wood, harrowingly identified. Something about the pattern of his thinking suggested this might be the time. It was a risk, both ways.

"Dear Emily,

I am writing informally, for we have spoken before, though never meeting, and I have always been pleased that you feel that those who review your concerts in my newspaper are sensitive and intelligent and fair.

I write with deep sympathy for the loss under tragic circumstances of your dear adopted daughter. My thoughts have been with you ever since the news broke, along with the thoughts of countless others, no doubt.

What I have to say now is perhaps obliquely related to your sad loss, but also to your well-known stand on political and social matters. My paper has had difficulty, as I have as editor, in steering a middle course between reporting the rather unusual doings of The Six and all that has happened to them, whilst remaining sceptical, and sometimes silent, as pressed to do.

My personal feelings, like those – and I have to say this – like those of most people – have hereto been a little scornful. Most of the other newspapers will continue to dismiss The Six as slightly mad. I am beginning to feel however, that I cannot in all honesty let my journal follow this course without putting forward an alternative line. And I myself – I am almost afraid to admit it, even to a friend in confidence - have begun to change.

I see my children, and think of all the children growing up in a world in which man's folly has polluted so much and even upset the weather. Will life be tolerable in fifty years' time, even without the wars being fought by so-called civilised nations, and the apparent impotence of politicians and of the churches to do anything to check bad trends, or even to bother enough?

Again, I am alarmed to admit it, I find in myself the beginnings of that caring pessimism which you and your friends see – paradoxically – as the only hope for us all.

I may say that I have been a fairly a successful press man, and I have no fond wish to confront the Establishment and put at risk my staff and myself. But I begin to think that the whole matter needs broadening out into wider public discussion, and - may I say this? – your personal tragedy has made this possible. There has been such a rush of public sympathy for you, so that much of the routine scorn and scepticism, as well as pressure from the top, has eased.

I would like to meet you to discuss the possibility of, perhaps a weekly newspaper series, or TV features, or something else. This would be to sail close to the wind in terms of the government, but I feel we should try. Your presence and inspiration as a public figure for whom there is much love and admiration, would be a key element.

When you can, let me know how you feel.

Yours ever,

Charles Pearson

(17)

Emily returned from the mortuary with Elsa. The business of identifying the poor, half-decayed body of the much loved foster-child had been spirit-breaking enough without the throng of people from the press, considerate up to a point, but still pressing. Rob and Stocky escorted the ladies to their car.

Rob was vexed by a confusion of reactions to all that was going on. First of course there was the awful shared grief. Then there was the admission, since he knew so much, that somewhere at the back of his mind he had known – known that Fred might die - that the baby might be another victim: and now, hardly to be mentioned since he knew it was coming, the death from the blow of the huntsman's horse of Vicky's lover. Sometimes he cursed, indeed often cursed, his ability to know. And he knew on another mental wave-band, that there would be a letter.

Within a week the news came of Mick's death, and the grief of the two women, with the episode of the hunt brought back into the media limelight, and with reminiscences of the as yet unsolved murder of a former archbishop added in - all this made a rise in publicity for The Six; although it was no longer six.

The reactions of the bereaved women were remarkably different. Emily, who had half expected her loss, after a couple of days of intense mourning, determined to continue the work of the group, and her career in music as part of this. The murder of her child was never explained: the absence of any ransom note led her to believe that the connection was her work for The Six. She was programmed to conduct Mahler's fourth symphony, which ends with a child's vision of heaven. She was persuaded to let a colleague take that concert.

Vicky, so close to Mick, perhaps too close, sank into a lethal depression. After a few days it was realised that her condition was serious, and a nurse-companion was found to look after her. Her illness brought the original six down to three, plus Stocky, who was in effect a fourth member.

The beginnings of something which had haunted them all and been rejected seemed now to have a new authority: a sense of failure and a wish to give up. They had achieved very little, and had been the cause of two and possibly three deaths.

And yet Emily and Rob, with their special insight, knew that there was something more. But it was hard still to believe in that. Until Charles Pearson's letter came to Emily's notice.

(18)

Pearson did not take her to his usual venue for meetings with business associates, but to an inconspicuous café in a side street. The manager found them a quiet table in an alcove. Emily looked at Charles Pearson. He is a good man, Emily concluded: on the verge of being elderly, but still powerful and vigorous. His strong physique and brisk manner suggested ruthlessness as required, but there was kindness and concern in the bronzed, lined face.

She felt hopeful, at ease.

"I am an elderly man," he began, with the hint of a smile. "I have been lucky with a young wife who gave us children whilst we were still young, and soon grandchildren. I have a daughter expecting her third child. We have all, with a few set-backs here and there, moved hopefully forward down the years making up a continually extended caring home. We have enjoyed so much. Without thinking, we took simple optimism as our guide." He paused. "But now, as I look at my children, and their children, in this violent, parched, war-ridden world of ours, I have begun to understand some of the things you and your colleagues have been saying."

He paused. There were tears in Emily's eyes.

"It's so good, indeed in a way comforting, to have someone strong and influential on our side," she said.

"I'm not all that strong," he said, "but I have a number of contacts, and my staff find out many things."

It was her turn. "We mustn't appear to be preaching," she urged. "People don't like it. Just the truth, as perhaps you can find it."

He took her hand. They were silent for a moment.

"I have preached!" he admitted, with a boyish grin. "When I was in the first flush of youthful idealism, some sort of Christian, I felt that the gospel had something to say to the state of the world. They put me on trial, and I took one or two services in small chapels. I soon realised then that my gospel was not what they wanted. I was supposed to save the world for Christ. It was all about personal sin. But I was interested in a social gospel, about peace and social justice. I just didn't fit. Anyway, eventually I came to something like your view of life. I was supposed to believe in a god who gave his own son to suffer horribly to save this world. But, looking round, I decided that this world is a poor sort of place, hardly worth saving. Badly designed. Everything depends on the destruction of everything else. That's the 'great chain'. And man, at the top of the chain is the worst. If a god wanted to save a world he might well have shown some sense, and chosen one of the thousands, or, millions, of planets which must support life, out there in the great void, somewhere better than this dog's breakfast of ours. It's awful. The ground base, the final reality, is suffering."

"Religion will be our worst problem," said Emily, softly.

"We shall have to take it on, with all the rest," Pearson said doggedly. "I have come to the conclusion now that our best move will be via a TV channel in which I have some interests, a TV series backed up by the newspaper."

They set to work. The idea emerged of a TV series of perhaps five or six (not too long) items. "Religion first," said Charles. "It will cause a lot of fuss and a lot of aggression. To start with that will either kill the series or set it alight. A risk I think we should take. At least we shall keep some of the thinkers and troubled people with us."

Emily felt that he was right. She remembered Elsa's quiet sharing out of concerns. In the first instance that hadn't worked, but perhaps the disciple idea would be renewed in a new context. "We can share things out," she said, "animal welfare, transport, education, and the arts. Let's finish with the great tragic world view, with the politicians challenged. Dare we?"

"In all this we must take soundings," Pearson replied, "and legal advice. And we don't want boring documentaries – we need pictures, films, maps, interviews with lots of people with whom viewers can identify. And a bit of humour, the comic side of man's stupidity."

"We can certainly help with all that," said Emily.

He looked at her. "Sometimes," he said, "I think we are mad, planning this. It may even lead to prosecution, even prison. I don't at the moment think so. We shall have to look so carefully at all the material.

"But, you know, it's for the children's sake isn't it? At least it is for me." She remembered her loss, and he took her hand. She understood. "They are the vulnerable ones today, little ones, and those unborn. I love my country, and we are taking advantage of its still relatively free tradition, although that's beginning to slip. Our decent nation is slowly going downhill."

"I am so grateful," said Emily, her eyes filling again.

He said, "It will be devilish hard work to sell in the teeth of commerce and politics, the idea that our life of the wrong sort of profit, and power, and competition and war, is slowly killing the world; and that despair, the truth about the whole show, is the point at which renewal and regeneration might start.

"We must work harder," he finished, "and we'll meet many times over the next few weeks, with my advisors and reporters. We shall need to consult, and consult. But it will all be for the children."

They remembered the children every day during the intense, and indeed hopeful, weeks which followed.

(19)

It was Tolstoy who came to the rescue of these worried people, as they strove to fashion a television series which had to convince people that the beginning of better things was to acknowledge the cruel chaos of life. The original notion of a four - or five-part series, taking in turn the special concerns of The Six (as they once were) now appeared too heavy and overwhelming. Two programmes might make the point without appearing to beat the public about the head. The conviction persisted that religion, so-called, should come first, controversially, but not to deny the best, and the sincerity, of many church activities.

Tolstoy had seen military service before embarking on the great novels which made his name, as well as later writings in which he rejected violence and called for forgiveness and love for all men as tokens of a genuinely religious life.

So Emily, Rod, Elsa and Pearson, too, began to see that an attack on conventional religion would be merely negative, and alienating. Tolstoy took a middle way, for which he was eventually excommunicated by the Russian Orthodox Church, having concluded that he didn't like churches or indeed governments. But he was still venerated for his testimony as to what he saw as the love of God in ordinary life. So the surviving members of The Six, and Pearson, agreed on a re-examination, not an outright rejection, of religion in the view of the dark truth revealed to them. "We have", said Rob, "to love the people whose feelings we hurt, and even as we hurt them offer some guidance and hope."

Stocky was, for the moment, taking a minor role in this planning. He had been visiting a tragically poor state abroad, where a young priest, whom he loved, was working in a church which was as much a place of healing and support for those oppressed by the state as a place for formal worship. Stocky, with surprising diffidence, felt at this stage that, as he had not been part of The Six from the beginning, they should choose the TV syllabus. But he wanted to be called upon, when the others felt it to be appropriate, in debate about certain aspects of religious worship. "Wherever I am," he wrote, "I am with you all the way."

The second programme, no less controversial, would deal with education and with politics, with global needs, war, and the general failure to develop clear and honest thinking. They would appeal for those qualities which teachers and statespersons alike ignore at their peril, and ours, creativity, imagination, and a feeling for the whole creative world in its suffering, an ability to recognise cant.

For this The Six had seen two die, and perhaps the third mentally, permanently, scarred. For the sake of the victims, the others wanted to use a new medium to deliver a message of despair and of hope.

But the best-laid schemes......... As Emily was to say later, "They've proved our case. Evil and suffering are endemic to life – how wrong it is to talk about a "Satan" or a "God," as separate and warring entities, when the destructive and the healing forces are for ever entwined in the fabric of existence, as the world has been made, or at least developed."

The little remnant of "The Six", as much as ever convinced of their constructive pessimism, now concluded that, in view of the forces ranging themselves against them, it was now the highest charity to compromise even more, to avoid confrontation as far as possible, to try to oppose hate and indifference with love. There was already too much absolutism in the world. It was felt worthwhile, and perhaps the most to hope for, to consider anew the position of men and women working and supporting their families in cruel occupations, and to pray for them to make even small modifications which might leave their basically cruel tasks a little less oppressive and horrifying to animals in their trust: so pushing back a little the cloud of darkness, letting in a gleam or two of compassion even in the midst of necessary oppression. Amelioration: that was to be the word now: all that could be hoped for in our time, until a global shift of consciousness towards a solemn recognition of the truth came about, long after the four of them were gone: a seismic shift in industry and trade: towards compassion.

But where cruelty was employed purely in the interests of sport, as an unnecessary hobby, as a sort of play, here it was felt that less effort was to be made to meet protests half-way. Only in this context would they now retain a sharpness of criticism, as it had been exercised by Vicky.

Pearson had worked hard. He had pulled strings with the TV company, pressing for a producer and a director who could in good measure identity with the ideas of The Six.

At a meeting with TV staff, rather more formal than earlier discussions, a change was felt in the climate. Pressure was put on Pearson and his friends to cut the two evening programmes to one. The TV magazine was about to go to press, and this amendment was reluctantly accepted. "They've been pushed," murmured Pearson, "but from where?" And then on the same evening another blow fell, as an edict arrived, to the effect that the whole venture was to lose feature status, and be reduced to a short item amongst others in a series called "Passing Topics", with a casual entertainment rather than a serious aspect to it.

Elsa and Rob were still staying at Emily's. The following night Rob woke with the impression that there were unusual movements outside. He rose to look around, but the back and the front windows yielded nothing. They still had two private security people. What Rob did not know was that one had left the site for a short time. Elsa was the first to rise in the morning. She screamed as she opened the garden door to feed the birds.

A dead sheep, bloody, lay across the step. Rob brought Elsa in, and went out himself, after counselling his distraught partner to keep Emily indoors. At the side of the house a young calf lay with its throat cut. It was dead, but gave the impression that it had been left to bleed to death. There was something on the front door – poultry, half-alive, two chickens and a duck, hanging by the legs. Rod recognised the discoloured, infected feet of birds which had been for ever in cages. Below them on the lawn nearby lay two cats, strangled with cord. Surely this was enough.

Rob, sick with horror, turned to the fourth wall, where lay a box of foul- smelling decaying fish. It was only later that he recognised the work of yet another industrial group. Across the front door the spray paint had left its ugly mark – "Dirty pacifists. Stupid conchies. Go to hell." "They are nearly all here," thought Rob, "all the groups we've offended."

But one last nexus, the transport lobby, had their revenge differently. In the morning's papers it had sponsored a full-page notice. It showed a glamourised gleaming car, and a crowd of happy people boarding a plane, with smiling attendants and a bronzed, cheerful captain. In the bottom corner a small split scene in darker colours showed a disgruntled crowd waiting for a late train, and an overcrowded bus. Below all this it ran,

GROW UP. BE MODERN. LEAVE THE PAST BEHIND. DEFEAT THE SICK CONSCIENCE OF THE SIX.

The missing security man was found in a field with a head wound. He recovered, but could remember nothing of the night's doings. Meanwhile his colleague left to get help. The local council was reluctant to help to clear the horror surrounding the house, but after a terrible day's delay it was taken away for recycling.

"When troubles come they come not single spies, but in battalions." Shakespeare had said it all. And then a phone call came through from Pearson. He seemed to be crying. "God! We're supposed to be a democracy! Oh, my dear friends, I've got to pull out. I've been warned – I can't even tell you who warned me – that if I carry on with my name on the credits my newspaper may be shut down. I can't do this to my workers, some of whom have been faithful colleagues for a very long time. To think that this was once a decent country! But what can you expect from an administration which supports illegal wars on flimsy excuses to please the military-industrial complex, and cares little for the lives it sacrifices. So the defence people have got together with all the other agencies which don't like your 'alternative' views. And yet in a way I am sorry for them. Their upbringing has never helped them to take on board the necessary tragic vision – that we are all trapped within a pre-determined system. Though, like you, I am not sorry for the cruelty for fun brigade, who could change things if they tried."

For a time it looked as if their TV appearance, their last effort to transmit the strange vision with which Rob and Emily had been blessed, or cursed, might now disappear forever. Emily, a titled person and well-known, seemed to be their last hope. She was too prominent to be bundled into obscurity. The loss of her child had not been forgotten. Also she had been advertised for weeks as conductor at a series of Mahler Festival concerts. She suspected that an attempt might be made to arrange a timetable clash between one of these commitments and the TV appearance. But "They" were either too slow or too scared to play that card. Nor were "these" powers quick enough to sabotage a radio gossipy morning programme, when she raised eyebrows for mentioning "problems" encountered by "some of my great friends and myself in exploring quietly and peacefully ways of making society gentler and more compassionate." Meanwhile two professors of music pulled strings to get her to stay on TV with her three friends. A few other friends, too, mainly from the world of music, stood up to be counted. Assurances were given that the short item, no longer a feature, would go ahead under strict guide-lines.

Twenty minutes only would they have, with a brief space left at the close for critical comments from the world of trade and politics. The four, grateful for a small offering, agreed to take five minutes each. At least they would have to keep to the essentials for their message.

This was on a Sunday. Weary with the fighting of battles, Emily turned to her friends, now including Stocky, who would be the last to speak. They were looking out over the town. "Just think," Stocky said, with feeling as close to ill-temper and exasperation as this kindly and patient man ever showed, "that today, untroubled by the law, thousands of people in hundreds of churches will be singing about love, praying, and promising to cast out their sins. A few of us, trying to open people's eyes to the evil of this world and bring back into it a little more love, and encourage a sort of active piety, are hounded by authority and turned into outcasts. 'It's a mad world, 'my master's!' "

(20)

<u>Presenter</u>:   WELCOME TO PASSING TOPICS

We offer the next item in our miscellany to four people who have been in and out of the news for some time. Many of us think that they are slightly mad. But our adventurous programme is giving them place.

They are partners, Elsa and Rob, together with Dame Emily, who will be well-known to many of you, and a one-time priest who wishes to be known, in spite of his several university honours and a former high position in the church, as Stocky – he has returned from work in Africa to take part in this programme.

I will add little by way of further introduction except to say that Dame Emily and Rob are the surviving members of a trio who believe that they have been given, for no obvious reason, some kind of revelation concerning our world: Rob after an accident: Dame Emily during her work as a conductor. A third person, an Archbishop, similarly affected, has died as the result of a disturbance at a gathering to discuss these findings. My other two guests, though without the special revelation which the other two claim to have been given, are, like them, convinced that they have something to say.

Some viewers will already be laughing at the term "special revelation", so often used by cranks. But we'll let these people have their say, briefly, limiting each to five minutes, with a brief come-back from one or two of their opponents.

Let us have <u>your</u> comments too; I might add that Elsa is a former overseas missionary, but has now resigned from that work.

Well, a bit of mild controversy is good for "Passing Topics", now and then, so over to you. Elsa speaks first.

ELSA

Thank you for watching. It's easy to laugh at our "special revelation". I don't blame you! You will understand a bit more if I explain it in terms of ourselves and animal life – my friends will be dealing with the big issues of education, politics and so on. We feel that we are in touch with a darkness which is usually concealed from us, and because we have seen it, we long to suggest some sort of amelioration, some easing, whilst recognising that some of it is bound up in the tragic pattern of life, in people's need to earn a living and support their families. I feel differently about cruelty for fun, as you will see.

Please forgive me for a list of horrors, which I shall make brief, missing many out. We are a decent, civilised nation. We tear calves from their mothers, and after birth, either kill them or and send them abroad in crates to doubtful deaths overseas, often without food and water. We raise chickens, ducks and turkeys in cages or in vast overcrowded barns where for a life-time they can never move freely – birds whose nature is designed for grass, water, woodland and sunshine. We condemn mother pigs to the brutality of the concrete-floor farrowing crate, metal bars often scarring their skin. We don't condemn as we should the harpooning of whales, intelligent and sociable creatures, who give birth as we do. We catch birds, often very beautiful birds, imprisoning them for life in tiny cages. We kill many other birds, as well as porpoises and dolphins, because we use fishing lines many miles long. I could go on but will not. These procedures fit a mass-production society, but they demean us. Priests, men of God, sit down at their Christmas tables and eat poultry meat from birds whose lives have been one long hell.

We are pleading for some amelioration, ways of killing, if killing there must be, less awful. It means imagination, identifying with the animals. It means looking round the nice clean supermarkets at so much on sale which is the result of suffering, like the neat rows of chickens in plastic bags.

I am inclined to speak less tactfully about that other dimension of animal suffering, caused by "sport". To go hunting and shooting wild animals for enjoyment, is just horrible.

I feel personal sorrow for the thousands of ill-treated and often abandoned cats, dogs and horses, the work of more insensitive, emotionally-deprived people. There one ponders the subject of poor education and deprivation of love.

My little talk may seem narrow or sentimental in contrast with the weighty issues of my colleagues. It isn't really. We all sense a low cry of suffering, a ground-bass, all round the world. It is always there. We should listen. Thank you.

DAME EMILY

As many of you will know, I am an artist, fortunate in being in touch with one of the greatest arts, the art of music. The nature of music gives us a clue to so much. It is enjoyable, relaxing and emotional, but it is also a strict sound system governed by its own rules. I see this two-fold function as a symbol of education as it should be – relaxing, creative, free (within reasonable limits) and an enrichment of life: whilst at the same time success, and certainly fine performance, involve clear, precise, analytical judgment and effort.

To fit in with the commercial and militaristic world of today, our education is heavily biased towards discipline and analysis, without the corresponding creative, cultural element. This is why, when the discipline and the pressure become too great or too unrelenting there is a violent reaction towards a kind of mindless anarchy, as we see in the vandalism and mindless violence of today. We complain about high levels of crime and overflowing prisons, but what has made criminals, so many of them?

Social deprivation, of course, exists within a society led by leaders who spend our money on ventures which might otherwise have helped to level out social inequalities. But also lacking has been the neglected side of education, the joy of the arts in all their variety, education for creative leisure, and finally that great gift, good parenthood: to put it plainly, and I do so without apology, the teaching of love, love of persons, the environment and beautiful things. But on the other side of education, strictness, discipline, the undue and debilitating emphasis on testing, is in itself failing. It should encourage clarity of mind, clear thinking, the ability to detect and reject prejudice, bogus, language bigotry. It doesn't do that.

I hope my rather dry comments will have a little more life to them if I apply them directly to life today. We have emotionally-deprived people, all too often without that precious sense of the beauty, sacredness and tenderness of life. This is the road to social violence, but also towards war. On the other hand we have people ill-equipped to discern the crooked thinking, lies and half-truths of politicians. In fact the way is clear for us to be hoodwinked without our realising it.

When I had my vision, I could see a dark future in which people with empty heads and empty hearts will be hoodwinked by militarist statespersons into wars and confrontations and eventually into the last war. At a miserable discount, will be the notion of a world community, in which the confrontation of individual nations, their obsession with separateness, might be properly contained. Because of this omission, the worst of the weapons people, who really run the world, will always be laughing all the way to the bank.

Dear friends, this is the darkness, this is what it's all about. Education has something to say, if only we would listen.

Thank you.

ROB

When I first recovered from the blow which was the prelude to the vision or revelation, whatever you care to call it, I thought, as soon as I was capable of thought, like many of you perhaps, that I had just been knocked silly. Later I compared notes with our late Archbishop, who gave his life for the sake of that vision, and with Emily, and we were at one with one another.

I remember staring into the blankness, full of stars and galaxies, light-years away, and thinking of the pathos and absurdity of Earth.

We are an insignificant blob. Our own star, the sun, is one of millions in our galaxy alone, and not particularly bright. And there are millions of other galaxies, but we spend our time in nonsense, with separate nations, artificial and ridiculous, threatening each other with frightful horrors. Our money, taxed from helpless people, goes on the endless re-duplication of these horrors, whilst our social services and our health services go to pot. We can't even afford drugs for simple pain relief or for care for the elderly, for the cash is wanted for missiles.

I saw all this madness, as well as the fouling of the world with muck and the "warming it up" towards its extinction. At almost every point, however, considerations of cash, of trade, sabotage good sense. For example take transport. The trains had survived for a century to become a sensible and increasingly safe way to travel around. Then they were dismantled, foolishly, and only fifty years later that folly, and the pollution on the roads, became clear.

There were attempts to revive some of the old railways, with their abandoned fine bridges, viaducts and tunnels. But politicians went on building roads, roads that were always more dangerous and more polluting. This was typical of much insanity. I could quote more. We live in a lunatic asylum. What we need is government with powers to reduce insanity, check wars, reduce pollution, save lives, as if we were members of one family.

We should not have any more children until the world is better. It isn't fit for them.

We should also vet our statespersons. Too many behave as if they were psychopaths, oozing confidence, apparent sincerity, charm, whilst without conscience or care for those they injure and kill. They ignore public opinion. They reverse policies for which they have been elected. They browbeat parliaments, so that in the end the common people are barely represented at all and their protests ignored. They are also served by officials who care less for the people they are supposed to serve than for their own careers.

My valued colleague will be speaking to you about religion. He will describe some traditional laws and dogmas about morality and sin, mainly sexual. Like me, he believes, now that he has left the church, that all the fuss about sex is a carefully-calculated smoke-screen behind which other sins, far worse, can carry on, without people being much bothered. We all know that sex is a tricky subject. But if I had a son or daughter thinking of a political career, I should be happier to suggest the running of a decent, well-regulated brothel. They might do some good, and almost certainly do less harm, than the average statesperson. There are some good people in political life. But in general terms it is a sink, and corrupt. We know that there are fiddles at local levels. At the crucial national and international level, all but a few leaders make efficient international co-operation impossible. They keep tension up. They must always have enemies. Their ethics are those of the school playground.

STOCKY

We have been criticised for being "against religion".

I feel I should start by saying that we all four have, in a meaningful sense, deep religious feelings. I left the church to find real religion, Elsa has been a missionary during her search for God, and Emily often finds in music an intense experience similar to religious insight, and Rob had an idyllic childhood with a sacramental quality.

My comments will be short and simple. I believe that there are two main reasons as to why religion needs re-defining in the modern world.

First, the created world, as science now perceives it, shows no sign of a loving and all-powerful creative god. It is wonderful, but also brutal, a dark drama, with one species preying upon another. At the top of the chain is man, fine, but also the most dreadful. The male sex delivers a testosterone-driven urge, important for reproduction, but its aggressive quality leads to violence, and then war, which is almost always driven by men. This is a fault in the evolutionary process that shows no sign of being the result of intelligence.

I agree with Rob that the world is no longer fit for children to be born into. The amoral evolutionary trend is driving Earth towards ruin. Evolution is a failure.

Secondly, I have to condemn unreservedly the churches who prohibit contraception. Their edict is grossly irresponsible. There are already too many people in the world. To frighten women into pregnancies which they may not even be able to make provision for is blatantly wrong. Every child should be wanted and loved. But in the developing world there are chaotic, sprawling families resulting from religious fear. The fear moreover, is contributing towards the world's over-population. It is unforgivable.

Indeed the risk of world disaster, even apart from global warming, as the result of there being too many people using up too few amenities, is another sign of an unplanned, rather silly evolutionary process; on top of which we have violence, loss, grief, disappointment - and death; and to corrupt us, carbon emissions and nuclear power and other dangers. It could have been so good. Perhaps it is: somewhere else. Here, there is little sign of sensible planning *from without*, and, to anticipate argument, I, for one, have not agreed to take any part in some sort of ethical experiment on the part of a god.

God, or good, must now come from us, from our efforts to make sense of a bad job, even to transform it, and do battle against the worst and the most repressive aspects of evolution.

In that struggle there is little use for dogma, which usually works against people. All great religions have been to some extent dominated by dogma and by books, and by law so enshrined. If law does not fit in with life, and the ban against contraception is one such, then it must be dropped. Edicts made two or three thousand years ago may not be applicable in today's world. Let us set ourselves free, not into anarchy, but into good sense, which is the companion of love.

William Blake, hardly an orthodox man, once remarked that when a family sits down together in love, Christ appears in the midst. This is not literal. It doesn't need to be Christ, but any great religious leader. However the message is clear; and that's what it's all about in the end.

Thank you.

PRESENTER

We agreed to transmit the statements you have just heard on condition that one or two people with opposite views might put their case. An industrialist and a priest will end this part of our programme with brief statements. They would like to be known as A. and B. and we shall not show their faces.

A. As a businessman I object strongly to the gloomy view expressed. I do a good, resolutely ongoing, industrial job. These people would put thousands out of work. And the cutting out of extreme or cruel practices, as has been suggested, would bring down profits considerably.

We need people to be happy and confident, go to work happy and believe in their future. If they don't, we may have strikes and go-slows, and so on. The system is here. It is non-reversible, and it should not be questioned.

The Bible said that man has put the beasts of the field under his dominion, and when it's necessary they may have to be used ruthlessly.

I want education to give children impetus, to be keen on science and technology. If they want to study music, or some useless subject like poetry, let it be on a Friday afternoon after they have studied important things which could turn them into good businessmen and businesswomen, and seekers after profit. And I do not want our national defences run down for the sake of a few loony people. The arms business is highly profitable to employees and investors. We must let our enemies know that they will be blown to bits and have their cities turned into radio-active ash-heaps, unless they take note of us.

B. As a priest of God I am saddened by almost all we have heard today. Take the problem of juvenile vandalism. You won't cure this by getting kids to play the violin or undertake dance lessons. The cause of most of this trouble is family breakdown and lustful loose living. Parents and their children must be taught the commandments of God and if necessary be punished for non-conformity.

I like a nice, well-planned school, where pupils sit in straight lines and train their memories and sit for the curative discipline of formal examinations. This made me what I am, and I am grateful for it. And there should be regular divine assemblies in every school to remind pupils of God's laws, to give thanks for His wonderful world, and be ready to acknowledge His mercy and His works in everything we see. The last speaker from The Six is blind to the moral fibre which has made our nation great. His wishy-washy morality offers nothing to a generation adrift and looking for something to hold on to. Religious dogma is the anchor which holds people to the truth, and we dismiss it at our peril.

Let us welcome the rich heritage of church history and church tradition, as a basis for clean, tidy children who will come to worship regularly, obey the commandments, and prepare themselves for an honourable family life, supported by the excellent commercial system, which is the nation's reward for hard work, unquestioning faith and obedience to the laws of God. And we should prepare to defend the country against other nations. They may, at our God's command, be subject to devastating military force.

Thank you.

PART 4

THE REVENGE OF THE STATE

(21)

They were to find again and again that in dark times there are often kindly souls willing to stand out from the rest, perhaps to take risks, perhaps not, but always ready with a word of comfort. They are angels in dark places. Stocky, who seemed to know so many people and had so many contacts, was the king-pin and healing centre of so much of this. There were other unexpected things.

As the television interview ended and the four were ushered out, an official (was he a security man?) said to Stocky in an undertone, "There are crowds gathering at the front, some hostile. I could show you a small emergency door at the back."

Stocky showed concern, but not surprise. With a warm gesture of thanks, he pressed coins into the stranger's hand, gave himself a false name, and asked their helper to ring for a taxi. Hesitantly the man agreed, leading them down little-used stairways; and then left, afraid to go forward, but promising to telephone.

They lingered for a time in doubt in a dusty room off a passageway. There were distant voices. "This is fun," Rob remarked, with a smile. "This is a repeat of our escape at the back from the nursing-home. Life is rounding itself off!" Elsa clasped his hand the more tightly. She was crying a little, without quite understanding why. When distant voices ceased, they crept forward down a stairway, then along another passage, until they were confronted by an emergency door. It was resistant, and they were alarmed by the noise. But when the door at last opened on to an unknown side street, there was a taxi.

If they were recognised, their driver showed no sign of this. Stocky gave an address unknown to the others.

They were taken to an unfamiliar part of the town, and put down outside a gaunt terrace house. When they were alone, Stocky, in an undertone, said, "This is an emergency plan. We must get you three out of town as soon as possible, while you hide for a time." (What about this man himself, Rob considered? As usual he thinks of others and doesn't think of his own safety.)

Then Stocky approached the house, which he seemed to know, and said, "This is a temporary haven. A priest lives here, one like me who can't stand his church. But he's taken a different line. Very bravely he has refused to give up a partner for the sake of his church, and with the help of a landlady, who is one in a million, the girl he loves lives here too. One day he will be discovered. For the moment the girl is just a lodger, as the world sees it. More to the immediate point, he's willing to house us, and then help you to get out of town."

"I can't." said Emily. "I have to conduct at the end of the week, and there are rehearsals."

"Then you will have to stay here, as safely as possible, until we can get you to join the others. You'll be much in the public eye," he added, "but use your own house as a base, and get back here as discreetly as you can. Keep your own security guards." After that he added, with the cheerful smile the others were used to and valued so highly, "We'll just have to see how things go."

"We must see Vicky before we go," said Elsa, and all agreed. She had been much visited, although there was no change.

"This will be dodgy," said Stocky, "but we'll use my friend's car – he has also agreed to let us use it to get out of town later."

They were welcomed as old friends into Father Thomas' house, with its wicked secret. The landlady, after a moment's hesitation, came forward to Emily, placed her arms around her, and said, "So sorry about the little girl. So sorry!"

Soon they were sitting down to a simple but ample meal, joined by a dark and beautiful girl who took her place next to Thomas, and by Meg, the landlady (no one seemed to know or care about her official title.)

It was a Blakean meal, with love in the midst. Within minutes there were no strangers present. All was warmth, acceptance, laughter, desire to help. This septet, odd though it would have appeared in the eyes of the world, were one and all aware of a profound peace, a fellowship unknown to so many in the formal, mechanical world: an island of peace. The close bond mutually shared between the surviving members of the Six, and with Stocky, flowed over into the easy and loving bonding of the other three.

Stocky was to remember that hallowed evening, and for long. One of its first moments of grace betokened their mutual escape from the world on to a level like one leading to the gates of paradise. It was Meg, who had gone to Emily's side, as they all first entered the home. The two women had hugged each other, and both had wept. Meg would never have described herself as an angel. She had left school at fifteen, married early, and in due season lost husband and a daughter. In widowhood she had had a struggle to survive. She had little or no intellectual pretension; but she had bonded at once in love and sympathy with a brilliant woman with public honours heavy upon her. There were no barriers. Simple loving Meg had none of the fear of the flesh so often evident in the dogma-ridden and status-ridden, unable to adjust to the demands of love. Emily and Meg had hugged one another with tears. Stocky had rarely seen Emily so openly moved before, through tears which were an easement towards the healing.

But one had to come down from the Mount. Thomas left to do some telephoning. "I think we may be able to help," he had said, as he left the table. "You people deserve a break," he added. "You have done everything to alert the public, everything possible for you, except writing."

(22)

He had ministered before coming to town in a remote and beautiful hill country. There he had, in the course of his pastoral duties, supported a member of his flock, a woman desperately grieving over the death of her husband, her devoted partner for many years. With the help of her daughter, and by involving the distressed woman in the work of his church, by way of healing, he had helped her through a period of depression.

It wasn't until the worst was over that he realised that there was an unspoken love between the daughter and himself.

It remained unspoken when he was moved to a town parish. (Had someone been maligning him in relation to either mother or daughter?) The separation was an agony. The mother, if she suspected, was in awe of the priest, and said nothing. Wrestling with his conscience, he agreed to write, in restrained and unremarkable terms. He did penance after penance for his "sin". He felt that God asked for total rejection of wicked passion, but he was unable, though imposing punishment upon himself, to make the break complete. The worst temptation came when the girl decided to end her village life by studying for a degree, at first at home, and then at college, full-time, in town. Of course "in town" was Thomas' new parish, and she wrote, with her mother's approval, for advice about lodgings.

One evening Meg heard him sobbing. She entered his room and placed her arm across his shoulder. The floodgates gave way: he wept in her arms uncontrollably. And told her all.

Meg, as he was to find out later, was both an ordinary and at the same time an extraordinary woman. Her version of "God" implied an indwelling spirit which saw charity as the only restriction upon a duty to live according to the ground and nature of one's own being.

She saw how grief and longing, though interspersed with many penances, were tearing this man apart, impeding his work as well. She pushed no solution at him, at first merely comforted him, and told him to listen to his heart, to God within. When one winter afternoon a taxi arrived, Meg admitted the girl, and left the two lovers together. Their first open avowal of love was at first almost overwhelming. They slept apart for two weeks, and then with Meg's knowledge, moved in together.

Thomas's life and work took on a new radiance, which began to lessen his guilt. How to help absolve others from "sins" which he himself had committed? *Only by re-defining definitions of sin.* He had always regretted the churches' obsession with sex, seeing his church as a wider social force in a bleak world. His mistress now helped him to move along that line. "My love," she had whispered, "we've had our lives condemned by people who do not know us, or our circumstances, or our time. Meg has taught me to look for God, or good, in ourselves. Thomas, how can love like ours be against the will of a good and loving God?" And day by day he worried less, and could do more, with stress relieved, to help others.

And now, in gratitude for the miracle which had entered his life, Thomas saw that the hill village which had helped him to find new life now might help others. Consultations between Thomas, his lover, and the mother back there in the dales, seemed to point a way forward for those seeking refuge. The mother knew of a recently-vacated shooting-lodge, (certainly long past its bloody and savage history) let out for a holiday home and suitably secluded. Set well back from the village on the fell-side, and screened by trees, it could function as a peaceful retreat.

The place was checked out, booked without an end-date for Rob and Elsa. Preparations were put in hand for comfort and convenience, even to the extent of arranging for a local lad to take up provisions and post every two days, "A simple lad. I've told him that you are writers and need peace and quiet. I don't think he will gossip, especially if you cross his palm with a little silver!"

Meanwhile a visit to Vicky revealed no change. The sight of their pal's passive face, such a contrast with the passionate, enthusiastic girl they all remembered, reminded her visitors of the continuing heavy cost of their campaign. Thomas agreed to visit her regularly.

And so two days after their arrival at the priest's house Rob and Elsa took affectionate leave of Emily, who was to join them within a week, and of Thomas and his partner, who had risked much for them, and Meg.

It was particularly sad to break up the party. Rob was oddly pensive. But there was, thought Stocky, a new glow about the face of his fellow-priest, the glow of an adventurer, risk-taker. One has to take risks to love, he considered. He recalled the timid responses of most church leaders to great events.

With Stocky at the wheel, Rob and Elsa set off out of town, as far as possible using little-known streets, until the green land opened out before them.

(23)

They slept a little in the car. Once there was a rain-shower. At length they found themselves moving up a rough track, round them rain-washed, far-distant hills, the air fragrant. They saw a slightly romantic, slightly run-down house with trees. It looked friendly.

A hand-written note conveyed a word of welcome.

Stocky saw them in and left, promising to bring Emily as soon as she could come, and undertaking to take a short break himself.

Left alone, the two lovers looked round. They relaxed, it seemed, for the first time since they had met. The world was no better. But, Rob, as the sadder of the two, had not admitted before that sometimes one had the sense of something better than the dead weight of wickedness which encumbered all men - something which did not fit in with his philosophy nor with his ideas about good and evil – a sense that something was working for them, some grace. It had come with the arrival of unexpected help; in that Elsa and he had met at all; and in the goodness of this country retreat.

Now, after carefully surveying the grassy landscape around the house, they went hand-in-hand for an evening walk. A path snaked up from the village on to the high fell, but passed not less than a hundred yards from the lodge. They climbed up to the top to see mile after mile of hill country, with only a hint of a motorway in the far distance cut through the hills, its noise unheard.

Elsa had always been shy, diffident. But she had changed. She pulled Rob into the long grass, removed clothing and made love to her man. "Oh God," she cried, "This is life! Rob, love, never leave me!" There on the height they had their heights. And Elsa said, as Rob held her close, "Tonight will be our honeymoon night. We've never had one!" (Why did he in that moment of ecstasy, suddenly think of love among animals, in far-away places?)

They wandered slowly "back home", delighting in the long grasses which had sheltered their love and were beautiful in the evening breeze and late afternoon light, dancing to and fro, ever changing in tone and colour. A fox crossed their path not far from the house. "Do you remember the fox family in Vicky's garden?" asked Elsa. Another echo of the past. The fox looked at them, and then went on, not over-concerned. "They know." she added. "He knew we would not hurt him."

Things had been prepared so well for their every need. There was a bottle of wine, and a cold buffet. An amazing stillness was almost tangible, familiar to those who leave city life suddenly for country quietness. A clock ticked. It was one of those sounds of peace which come at least once in a lifetime for those who live in hope.

Afterwards they dutifully tidied the room, and washed dishes, closed downstairs windows and locked the outside doors. The moor was bathed in an almost violent orangey glow. They took hands and went upstairs.

There was an unspoken feeling that they would take their time. Time was so precious. They were beyond rushed hectic, tightly-timed life. Beyond modern civilisation. Beneath its apparent complexity, its apparent optimism, lay a kind of panic. They would reject that.

Elsa had known little physical love before she knew Rob. But she had learnt quickly, in part because of her growing belief in the spirituality of all life. She learnt more, as at first he lay and let her enjoy him. There are so many points, muscles, nerves, even far away from the familiar sexual places, which can grant soothing, healing and sharply relaxing pleasures. Many, including married folk, do not know them. How much better Elsa thought, how much more peaceful the world might be, if more people considered the wonders of their own bodies, as better than property and money.

The peace between them, intense, yet immensely calm and calming, merged imperceptibly into a need to be as one within a shared eternity. So Rob took the woman he loved into his arms and gently entered her. Both were taken aback by the sudden access of joy. Sex is best with someone you love. They moved slowly, steadily, until the moment when they came to the peak together. The Mount had been gained, though half the church people would not understand that. And then it was time to savour another intense and loving peace. They lay in one another's arms, and the world for the moment could call on others for help.

"Our honeymoon," whispered Elsa. "We've slept together before, but that was – a cracker!" He was pleased by the sudden comic colloquialism. She had left behind in the world the humourless seriousness of her old faith. Suddenly he said, "You took the pill didn't you? We can't – I'd dearly love it – have a child. The world grows ever darker. It isn't fit for kids anymore." She crept closer. "Don't talk politics now. It's the work of the miseries!" And they were both silent.

Over the next day or two they saw few people. Once a party of ramblers left the path up the fell and approached the lodge. "We gather that this is an old hunting-lodge. We are antiquarians. May we just take a look?" Most remained outside, but one or two came inside to view the high ceiling, the beams, the fireplace. A woman came to thank Elsa, smiling,

One morning they saw two dark figures, black against the green, ascending the fell from the village. It was a little too soon to expect Stocky and Emily. Two men came and stood before their door.

They were neatly and formally dressed in dark, narrow pin-striped suits. "I am very sorry," said one, polite, neutral. "You must come with us."

They knew at once that the government had broken up their peace. "No point in trying to escape," said the second man, gruffly. "We have other people all over the fell."

The lovers collected their most personal belongings, looked again at the quiet sitting-room, listened to the ticking of the clock, and left.

(24)

A few curious villagers saw them placed in a black car. They were driven back to town and put into what resembled the security wing of a large prison. They were left for a long time without food and drink. Then a man appeared, with a guard. His utterly nondescript appearance, they recalled afterwards, together with his quiet tone, seemed more menacing than any kind of aggression.

"You are detained," he said, "under regulations relating to public order. There may be a trial, but under special dispensation the government has the power to deport you."

"But why?" asked Elsa, dry-eyed.

"To defend democracy."

"This is nonsense," Rob cried. "We have been trying to encourage debate, and alert people to greater gentleness, kindness."

The man did not reply.

"What about Dame Emily?"

There was a long silence.

Then Rob said, "I do hope she will be kept separate from all this. She is a splendid person and means a lot to the nation. She has suffered enough."

Again silence.

Then the man spoke. "Dame Emily is dead. There has been an incident at a concert."

At once, Rob thought, who has been responsible? The details of her concert programme read like a forethought.

The first part of the concert had been genial, even light-hearted, but after the interval Emily conducted a performance of Gustav Mahler's Ninth Symphony, the last symphony he completed in full, after a dark time when he had encountered professional hostility, suffered the death of a young daughter, and learnt that he suffered from an irreversible heart condition. It was a valedictory work, almost a farewell to life.

Emily had fashioned the long first movement with loving care, leading through reminiscences of past times, moments of celebration, interspersed with sudden reminders of the waiting dark and ending in a wistful farewell. The dance movement which followed wasn't a happy dance. It resembled a sad comment on the emptiness of worldly pleasure-seeking. But its cynicism and despair was as nothing set against the ferocious *rondo-burlesque* which followed, surely a hectic picture of our feverish, corrupt world of greed and selfishness, ultimately self-destructive. Emily had once likened it to the mad crowd in Shelley's last unfinished poem, The Triumph of Life, which celebrated a blind-folded leader. In Mahler's hands, for a few moments only, the bitter stress gave way to a tender love theme, only for this to be mocked and perverted before the mad riot ended violently as it had begun.

After this horrifying vision of the future the audience seemed prenaturally silent.

The final extended *adagio* opened with a hymn-like theme, ironically a changed version of the horror theme from the *rondo*. It was then that Dame Emily appeared to be most deeply moved, as the slow movement witnessed to so many things which would never return, at times in quiet ecstasy, at others with a hopeless gesture as from the depths. She led her players and her audience through what seemed to be a brief retrospect of their own lives, until, with clash of cymbals, Mahler brings to a climax an underlying thankfulness for times past.

After that the *adagio* sinks gently and slowly down towards a last goodbye, the sleep of death. But this time that was not to be. During the last calm beauty of that farewell, the concert hall was shattered by a vast explosion. Most members of the orchestra, with their conductor, were trapped under part of a collapsed roof, whilst the front of the auditorium became a tangle of twisted wood and metal.

Who was responsible? The press, most, blamed terrorists who had been intermittently threatening the city for weeks. Rob suspected that the Government might have been involved. How had the explosive been placed?

Members of the audience, and all the players, had been carefully checked. The whole place had been under scrutiny. Rob had the impression that the bomb might have been placed under the platform, close to Emily's podium.

If so, it would have been the act of a Government afraid of change, anxious to target the most distinguished member of a group with new ideas.

Rob was comforting Elsa when Stocky was permitted to join them for a moment.

The three had another uncomfortable night in cells. In the morning, after a sparse meal, they were told of their approaching exile by way of a plane chartered for them. "Better than a trial," said one of their guards, but not with much sympathy. They were driven in a closed van to a remote airport which appeared to be little used. There was however a small shop, and the newspaper headlines, "Terrorists destroy concert hall," "Villains show hatred for good music." This would be the official line.

There was at least more comfort in the plane. When they asked where they were bound, again there was no reply. Elsa slept, exhausted. The middle-aged woman who served meals to them showed some concern for Elsa, who could not eat much. The woman had a kind face. "They've taken off the young and pretty ones," joked Stocky, when she had gone back to the kitchen. But this time the joke did not seem to work.

They were put down, after many hours, at a dusty, even more run-down, airport. They were driven into a town and on to a kind of tenement block on the outskirts. The surroundings were dismal.

A single white man came forward. As if he was dealing with some sort of objectionable material, he said, "I am in charge here. But you won't see too much of me. There is a native man here, my deputy. He can speak your language. He will settle you in. You must be within the building at night. You may go into town during the day if you wish, but don't try to escape. The coast is carefully watched. No one in the town is permitted to serve you with any food. You will eat here."

Hostile to the end, he motioned to another man who was standing a little way off, and left. The other man came forward. They knew at once that he too, had been a victim. "Come with me," he said. "I must not be seen to be too close to you." The white man's car was leaving. "I will talk more to you later." They were led inside the dismal building and shown two rooms on an upper floor. Each room had a couple of chairs and a bed and a small table. There was no carpet. The air was hot and stuffy. They were in the tropics, and from what could be seen through the barred window, they were not in an area designed for a holiday resort.

Elsa sat and cried. She had accepted some simplicities of life during her time as a missionary, but nothing as gloomy as this. Rob was thinking that perhaps Emily's death had been a blessing for her.

She could have coped, or again could not have been expected to cope, with this new predicament. Was this why she had been killed? They waited miserably and apprehensively for their first meal.

After a silence, Rob said, in a strange tone, like that of a prophet, "It's all right. For us, I mean. We shan't be here forever. I know. I have known all along that our efforts in our own country would fail. I felt I should not tell you, because it was good for us to try. Now I know that we shall go from here. I see that Stocky will go south to a great city. And for my love and myself, I have felt for years that our final destiny will be amongst trees, woodland, perhaps jungle. But I don't know how we will get there. But we will." He paused. "But over all, of course, I see the blackness I saw so long ago. The dreadful suffering". Meanwhile, he went on, in something like a normal chatty voice, "Let's decide, now, and specially when we get out of here, to enjoy what's left of life, we, the lucky ones, who may be imprisoned, but are not yet starving, or being tortured, as so many others are. We have been working so hard. It will not be wrong, but right, to take time off from stress. There may be more tasks ahead. But these I do not know. But puritans have done as much harm as militarists. Let's relax and enjoy."

There was a knock at the door. "At least we have that amount of courtesy," said Stocky. Their guide entered. He was thin and worn, simply but neatly dressed in the slightly convict-style dress which most people there seemed to assume. He paused a moment, and three pairs of eyes met his. Something passed between them, and Rob, especially, knew that they had a friend.

There wasn't much sitting-down space. In the end they got him to sit on the bed.

He seemed amazed by even this show of courtesy.

"I have a few routine things to tell you," he said, "You will be insulted if I welcome you - this isn't that sort of place. But I have let the others know a little about you – that you, like them, are victims of government. There will be no hostility. I have put you together at the end of one table. Once a week we all help to clean the dining-room, and we all get some pocket-money. There is a sort of little snack bar and sweet trolley on that day, too. It is safe to drink out of the plastic water containers, but don't drink from the tap."

"You said, 'government'," said Stocky.

"I must explain," said their visitor. "By the way, this is one of three settlements. This is mainly for the single and the elderly. There is another for families with children. But we have all suffered. I am glad that I am able to talk to you in your language. On the other island I was the only one studying, and I have been able to carry this on here."

Stocky said, "'the other island'?"

Elsa was staring intently at the visitor, her voice suggestive partly of fear, and of a kind of affection for him. Rob was silent: nothing would surprise him. But their visitor seemed unable to go on. Suddenly he said, "I know your names. May I use them? And will you call me Dave? It isn't my name, which you'd find difficult, but I believe people from your country often call each other 'Dave'."

For a man strange to them from an unknown race to choose a shortened name, which might have been used in a close family circle, or pub, or club back home, was hilarious, or should have been. In the circumstances, and especially in view of Dave's obvious agitation, it was not.

"I haven't told you about everything," Dave said, "as the people I meet know it all too well. Forgive me if I hesitate."

"All the people here have lived on a small island, almost too small to be on small-scale maps. We were an easy-going community, living mostly by fishing. We had dogs, which were more than pets. They were trained to enter the sea and catch fish for us. We had no parliament. In case of dispute, a small group would get together to sort out the trouble. Because I was the one studying and had taken a correspondence course, people looked to me as a kind of leader, or spokesman. It was a simple way of life, and we were very happy.

"Then one day we were told that your government, which was responsible for us but had usually forgotten us more or less, had been asked by a super-power to give up our island. The big chaps wanted it for a military staging-post. Your nation just handed it over without question, with no thought of the consequences for us. There was apparently no discussion in your parliament. The whole thing was decided behind closed doors, by secret edict.

"One day a foreign cruiser lay off our little island home. A great ugly thing. We were told, at gunpoint, to collect a few belongings, leave our homes, and board small naval vessels to take us to the big ship. Our dogs, to our sorrow, were rounded up and destroyed: gassed. People who resisted were roughly handled. We were brought here to be put in these lodgings with a pittance to live on. And that is our story." He was weeping.

Elsa ran to comfort him.

He went on, "The people here do not like us. Our children go to school; but they are not treated well. It is all very sad. We miss our homes. One or two people died of sadness." With an access of anger Dave added, "Now I believe, the intruders have all they want

– an airfield, fine homes for service men and women, clubs, a sauna, a chapel!"

Stocky spoke for us all. "This is dreadful. Governments! As usual most of the big things they do are immoral and illegal. And they do not care."

"And they lie," said Dave. "We were told that we were not the real original race there and that our island was in danger of flooding because of global warming. All lies."

A bell rang for the evening meal. Dave tried to settle them down, but the food was plain and Elsa could not eat much. Their fellow prisoners smiled a little but no more. Except when they were leaving - an old woman came up to Elsa. She had been crying, and Dave had to translate. She says, "She misses her dog so much. He was her best friend."

"We must do something," said Stocky, later. Then to Rob, "You knew it all, didn't you?"

Rob's reply was, "It proves us right. The world is a sink, run largely by villains. Our dark visions were true."

(26)

Dave showed them the local shops, where they could buy stationary as well as various personal items, but not food. Once, they managed to smuggle in wine, which they shared with Dave.

"There is a little park nearby, with a distant view of the sea," Dave told them.

Occasionally post arrived. Father Thomas wrote about Vicky - there was no change. There were one or two letters from sympathetic priests, friends of Stocky's. No one was quite sure that all the post was getting through. One letter from a parishioner for Stocky was addressed to "The Very Reverend Dr....." The details on the envelope were noticed by one or two people within the complex, and without.

A few days later, Stocky received a note from the island's Assistant Consul. It suggested a private, very private, meeting. The lines of old comradeship stretched far, he mused. The A.C. had been a university friend. "No idea he was here". The appointment would be most unusual, against protocol, but might be arranged, with due care. The old boy network was hinting at a force working for good. A few days later a closed car picked up Stocky near the park.

Stocky was ushered into Charlesworth's presence by a secretary who looked at his clothes with suspicion. They were now in a better part of town. "Don't worry about my assistant," Charlesworth said. "I know enough about him to keep him quiet." Then, "You were Stocky in those days, and then you got clerical weeds – and now here you are again!" His friend had now, perhaps, a little too much flesh on him. But their suddenly renewed friendship was good on both sides.

After a sherry or two and a general résumé of Stocky's career since university days, Charlesworth said suddenly, "Dammit, we must get you and your friends out of here." And then in a lower voice, "And I wish I could help the other poor devils as well. I've been ashamed of what my country did. Felt impotent about it. I have a very good boss, but he always toes the party line." He mused again. "Got to get you out to the African coast, if we can. Will be in touch."

Stocky looked again at the fine apartment, the whisky, the sherry, the fine furniture. Being Stocky, he said, as they were about to part, "Don't take any risks on our behalf. We don't want help at the expense of the welfare of an old friend of mine." They shook hands without saying much more. "I'll have a think," said the A.C. "And we'll meet again."

As Stocky was taken back towards their gloomy residence he felt a shift in their fortunes. They had found another friend.

Stocky was guarded when discussing the interview. He was anxious not to raise his friends' hopes too high.

Meanwhile all three went on writing. The tri-partite authorship was unusual, but they knew each so well that it began to take shape, a three-fold autobiography beginning with early days, outlining false judgements and false leadings from prominent figures.

They went out sometimes to the little park, and gazed over the houses towards the distant sea. One of the local shop-keepers occasionally slipped them a little extra food, a few fancies.

At last the note arrived from Charlesworth. No doubt for good reason, the A.C. did not want another meeting in his office. He suggested a word in his car parked at the park near his friend's "residence".

He came to the point quickly. "I want to get you three out, and I have plans. I have a boat – a small craft, but capable of ocean-going – I have leave coming up. I'd like to smuggle you aboard".

"We aren't allowed out at night after nightfall", Stocky reminded him," and there are guards about to stop us leaving."

"I've thought about that", Charlesworth went on. "This is a risky business, and if anything goes wrong, I know nothing about it – do you understand? Sorry to be so spineless."

"I understand."

"One Sunday soon there's a festival, a sort of carnival – centred on the harbour. It's very jolly and a bit over the top in the evening. Everyone will be there, including the police. Could you get out somehow?"

"We could try."

"With any luck the quiet part of the coast-line nearest to you will be more or less unguarded. There's a small jetty close to a place where they repair boats. I can give you a key. With any luck you could get out under cover of darkness. If you're discovered before you get to the boat, make up some story about looking for a doctor. I shall know nothing about it until we are on the open sea".

"It's worth a try. You are so good to us. One thing though. I'd like to bring Dave, the one who has been so good to us, the scholar amongst the other people."

"I don't know. There's not a lot of room. But – damn it - I was going to tell you. I shall be bringing a woman, a damn fine woman. Not my wife. She left me some time ago. Do you mind? Though at university you were always a liberal sort of parson."

Stocky laughed. "Do you really think I'd bother, or judge you? The whole sex thing has been blown up by the churches to hide from us so many of the other sins, war, commercial exploitation, lack of care for the land. That's why so many religious fundamentalists have subtle links with industry, including the arms set-up. For goodness' sake old pal, bring anyone you like, bring a tame hippo! Unless we get all these silly sexual judgments out of our hearts and minds we shall go on having wars 'for peace'. Excuse me for going over the top. To think that politicians can condemn stem-cell research, or contraception, when no harm is being done, no cruelty to a being, whilst they are planning wars and thousands will die. Religion drives men mad!

"Remember Voltaire, 'Atrocities are committed by those who believe in absurdities.' Sorry to go on! I have always felt that church leaders who go on at full blast about sex and ignore so many other sins, exhibit rationalised laziness. And not to take risks and not get into trouble – that's the line! I seem to remember that Jesus took risks."

"Wow, you certainly feel strongly about that. So I needn't worry about bringing Mirielle? I can assure you that stranger things go on in the white community here."

(27)

It was agreed that Mirielle would act as a sort of decoy, if needed in that capacity on the night of the escape.

Things moved with unexpected speed. The weather played its part, remaining calm. Dave refused to go with them, feeling that he had to stay with his own native friends: but he wished to help in every way, agreeing to take a warning call from Charlesworth when the critical hour had arrived, letting the three out, and promising (this was begged of him by all three) to avoid any threat to his own position.

There was no moon, but the chosen night was warm and fine. A call came through on Dave's phone – the only one allowed on the campus. They left through a side door, discreetly left unlocked, some little way from sleeping-quarters. Rob, Elsa and Stocky were torn apart to be leaving so many unfortunates unable to get away; but they were supported by their promise to Dave to write and press the case of the oppressed people in every way possible, and by a comment from Charlesworth – "Can't do anything while the Chief's in office, but when he goes we'll start pulling strings - by means fair or foul!"

They each embraced "Dave", who left quickly. Keeping as far as possible under the shelter of trees, they made their way down towards the small ferry-port where a few boats were under repair. They were almost there when they were startled by the shape of a woman moving towards them, but she whispered, "I am Mirielle. I have looked round. I think we are safe to board." They ran along the jetty. "You will know the boat by its name!" the girl had said. "Atlantis."

Soon they had the door unlocked and were in. The sound of a car worried them, but it was an official car bringing Charlesworth. It was a moment to remember when he joined Mirielle and the others, and all seemed well.

The A.C., dressed informally for the occasion, seemed a different man. Happy and excited, he embraced his woman warmly, and then congratulated the others on their escape. "By the way," he added, with a grin, "don't worry about the absence of extra crew. Better to be on our own. I have a full pilot's licence, and have done this trip before, sometimes in heavier seas. You three must have the little dormitory accommodation."

Stocky protested. "We're the lucky intruders. We'll sleep anywhere – the deck, the galley!"

"Nonsense," smiled Charlesworth. "Mirielle and I will be up on the bridge, as we call it. We shan't sleep much. Plenty of time for that tomorrow! And I think we should be getting away."

Rejecting any further protests, the A.C. and his partner disappeared to the upper level, and soon the engines were purring. After a warm-up period which pushed up the anxiety level briefly, everyone felt the boat moving gently out to sea, and then accelerating into the ocean.

For the three below, relief brought on sleep. Soon after first light Mirielle appeared with morning tea. She was tall, dark, not unlike Thomas' mistress, but far more overtly sexual. Rob remembered Shakespeare's Cressida:

> *There's language in her eye, her cheek, her lip,*
> *Nay her foot speaks: her wanton spirits look out*
> *At every joint and motive of her body.*

And what was wrong with that? She was also kind. Elsa was all he wanted, but Rob, clear now of old destructive puritanism, rejoiced for his friend.

Mirielle brought maps. It seemed that once again the three were about to acknowledge the presence of a special grace.

They were to land at a sizeable town with a railway which would carry Stocky south to join his friend in the industrial belt. Moreover the port was familiar to Elsa. Twenty miles north lay the small coastal town where she had worked as a missionary. An old contact might point them on their way.

The party of five did not dally at the port. "Don't worry," said Charlesworth, "I don't think anyone here will know you three. And if they look at anyone it will be Mirielle." That was certainly true! The A.C. was well-known, and formalities were minimal. They took a cab to the town centre. Close by was the railway station. "I and going to leave you three here, now," said Charlesworth, "but I hope, one day, we shall all meet again."

Onlookers, mostly natives, were interested to see five white people, the sort who usually parted with a luke-warm hand-shake, warmly embracing, and for rather more than a split second. Future tactful communication was going to be difficult. They discussed various possible channels, before the A.C. and his lady left for their hotel. Shakespeare, Rob thought, had it again:

Hereafter, in a better world than this,
I shall demand more love and knowledge of you.

Stocky was to take a train south in an hour's time. A financial crisis had been averted by Charlesworth, who had pressed money on the other three. "There's plenty more where this came from," he insisted. They had been relying on their regular pittance. Between really close friends there is little embarrassment about money. It was a commodity, like food or coal, "One day we'll pay it back," said Rob.

When they saw Stocky off they felt the closing of a book. They had all been through so much together. Elsa and Rob were both in tears. But Stocky was to go to work, and spread kindness, with the man he loved.

Rob and Elsa waited in a little café for the afternoon bus which would take them north. The journey, when it came, was crowded and uncomfortable. There was land which had been cleared for commercial growth; and then forest. Their route took them for a time close to the coast. Elsa was saddened to see, as before, whalers out to sea.

(28)

The little town where she had once been sent to preach the word of God didn't seem much changed: but Elsa was acutely aware of the change in herself. How could she have believed such things, and ignored so much? She was now a new person.

They left the little bus uncertain of their next move. There was a petrol station, where, Elsa remembered, a friendly man used to manage a joke or two. But the place had been taken over by a larger company and re-furbished, and staff changed. They asked one or two people about a nearby animal shelter, or something similar, but without success.

Then Elsa felt that a brave, if desperate, throw was needed in the shape of a visit to the home of the head of the church where she had once ministered. It had been managed by a man calling himself "Padre", as an officer in the army of the Lord – a term more militant and aggressive than "parson" or "bishop". His house was much altered now, a fine detached dwelling in a run-down part of the town.

The Padre was, as usual, overpowering. "So it's Elsa! So glad to have you back! So much work to do in this evil town! We are soon to have dinner." Then, to his wife, who was somewhere in the background, somewhat overborne, "Lay two more places. You'll like my new house. I live in the midst of my flock, always ready to guide and warn, and listen to confessions. There's sin everywhere! It's a straight and narrow path, the good life. I have to keep my flock away from monstrous sins."

They decided to adopt a less than honest stance for the moment, for the sake of a greater good. They were both aware of monstrous sins, but not those occupying the closed mind of the Padre.

"We need you to help to clean up this place. Sex outside marriage, homosexual pleasure, contraception, abortion, people stimulating themselves, even with mechanical toys, oral sex, under-age sex, and so much more. The church continues to be a shining light to lost souls. Some are in our own congregation! So I hold regular repentance sessions for weeping and repentant sinners. They are really great to witness! You really must come back, sister. Can you take up the Lord's burden on Monday?"

"I'd like to ask for your advice, Padre."

"Splendid, splendid! I am always ready with good advice."

"We are both interested in the plight of animals, domestic and wild. Do you know of any organisation near this town which cares for animals, perhaps a sanctuary, or shelter?"

"That would be a side-line to your work here. No, I don't know much about animals. God put them under our feet. Scripture says so. They are here to be used. Animals have no souls, you know."

Not interested, he returned to his usual obsession. "We humans all have to be saved. I target the young. Tell them that sex can be the agency of the Devil. I preach abstinence."

His gaze shifted casually towards Elsa's fingers. "A lovely stone, to sanctify your union. Tell me sometime about your wedding. Perhaps you have photographs. I suppose you will stay overnight. We now have a pleasant guest room."

They had got no help. To continue with deception seemed ignoble.

Elsa said, "Padre, Rob is a wonderful partner for me, and we have been working with others to alert people to suffering, to try to spread a spirit of love, a concern, as in your way, you have a concern too. We don't want to deceive you. Rob and I aren't married, though we are utterly committed. I cannot help you in your work here because I have changed my view of things."

The padre's eyes, which had been ever-widening, now blazed forth. He stood up, over-turned a dinner-plate, and shouted, "Not married? Living in sin? Get out of my house. You'll pollute it!" His wife made a move as if to speak, but he added, "Do not bother about that guest room. Turn them out."

The wife said to Elsa, "Have you anywhere to go for the night?"

"Let them go to a brothel, or the town's rubbish dump. Or let them sleep on the streets."

"Dear, it isn't very loving to just turn them out. Can they sleep on the couch, just for one night?"

The moral man swept out, banging the door. It was the wrath of God.

Elsa was crying, deeply hurt by the ferocity of the man for whom she had once given so much. The wife drew near. "There is an animal sanctuary a few miles north. I don't know why he didn't remember that. I know a man with a car who would take you there before he begins his usual working day. Sleep down here, and leave early with him. I will telephone him, and the animal place also. This taxi-man is a good friend, and he will come to get you out of this house." There was a sort of sob in her voice.

"You are very kind," said Elsa, taking her hand. It didn't seem the time or place for close physical contact. "We are sorry to have caused you distress. We have rejected your husband's faith." The wife said nothing.

The car arrived. The Padre's wife, alone, saw them off. She ventured a slight wave.

Later, Rob said, "Did you see her face when we left? I think she was a little envious."

(29)

Their driver said little. For their part they were too tired after an uncomfortable night to try conversation. At length the taxi-man pulled up the car in what seemed like a remote part of very dense bush.

"Can't turn round down there," he said, pointing down a side track. "Watch out for snakes." Rob prepared to pay him for the rough going and the early start, but the driver resolutely refused all payment, although much pressed. "She's paid me," he said, and left abruptly, as if a little hostile, or embarrassed.

They went hand-in-hand down the track, which, though narrow, showed signs of vehicular use. It seemed to go on forever, and for a time Elsa began to wonder whether this was going to be the way to get rid of them finally. Then, at a turn of the path, they saw a high stockade, and a stout gate, beyond which two people were waiting to receive them.

They both admitted later to a strange sensation of being at last once and for all at home. Gerald ("Don't call me Gerry" - I had enough of that at school"), a broad-shouldered man of perhaps fifty, with humour over-lapping the lines of worry on his face, introduced his partner, Flo, younger, warmly physical, who embraced both visitors. "You're not visitors," said Gerald. "We know about you, and hope you may intend to stay. We can do with some help. Come and have breakfast. I suppose the parson's wife got you here. I've seen her about sometimes in the taxi. God knows she needs some relief from the heavy man she lives with."

They were moving over a seemingly limitless grassy area, over which elephants, many of them, were scattered, along with a few other animals. "See that little one all by himself by the stockade," said Gerald, addressing the newcomers, as if introductions were already over. "That little chap has seen his mother shot. We found him by her side, bewildered and distressed. I'm almost a pacifist these days, but if I could get hold of the people who do this sort of thing, I should be pacifist no longer. The little chap is still grieving. He will not mix with the others. Dora will do all she can."

Elsa and Rob were aware of a large elephant approaching, then moving alongside. "This is Dora," said Gerald, "our oldest inhabitant, and one we could hardly manage without. She is supremely intelligent, very loving, and, really, a friend."

As the great beast drew near, Gerald and Flo drew a little apart, as the other two were a little apprehensive. Dora advanced, halted, and very gently extended her trunk, wrapping it round Gerald and Flo in a gesture clearly of profound affection. They stroked and patted her huge flank. When the elephant had released them and began to move away a little, Gerald said to the newcomers, "She will come to love you too. These animals have a great range of feeling."

The four were now approaching a ranch-type house set above the forest floor. "We'll talk over a meal," said Flo.

Their talk was plainly spoken, forthright. The animal refuge had been in the care of an elderly couple who had used their very considerable income to work towards the relief of animal suffering, in days when such philanthropy was unusual, even eccentric. When they were too old to continue, Gerald and Flo, until then in government service and pressing their rulers with little success to take notice of animal welfare, were asked by one of the animal relief charities to take over. They were now being supported by two or three voluntary bodies, one from a liberal religious foundation, aided by a bequest from the previous owners. But the income was by no means certain. "If you come to work here," said Gerald, "it will be a bit of a risk." It was agreed that Rob and Elsa would share that risk.

"We have TV here," Gerald went on, "though it's a poor picture and sometimes goes off! This is part of the way in which we know about you. We admire your efforts tremendously. We can't offer you much except pocket money, but all the rest will be found. We have by the way our own power-supply – one of our native helpers is a brilliant electrician."

There were, it appeared three native helpers who had been offered full board and live-in arrangements with everybody else, but they preferred their own quarters behind the house. "They are splendid people and 'with us all the way'." They were invaluable, it seemed, when it was necessary to go out into the forest to rescue animals.

Elsa and Rob felt they had now come home. When they could they would continue their writing, otherwise happy to work at the simplest tasks in the interests of love and pity, in a place which they could come to love, and one which Rob had always known of.

As they prepared for sleep on their first night in the forest, Elsa noticed, not for the first time, a moment or two of introspection in Rob, withdrawal, which left her a little disturbed. In this there seemed to be hints of their first meeting. When she mentioned it, he said, "It's as if we've come round in a sort of circle, as if I'm back to something like that darkness we talked about long ago. But of course, it's absurd, when we have so much to be thankful for, when so much time has passed."

The relationship between the four of them was so naturally easy that the transition from being newcomers to being helpers was swift and effortless. Indeed Gerald and Flo were like the parents the other two had lost; and this in spite of Flo's being not so many years ahead of the other two. She had been Gerald's secretary in days before they both opted out from political life, which, to be fair, was sometimes well-intentioned, at other times more often a matter of bowing to outside interests and internal policies largely irrelevant to common people. Now with their friends' help they pulled a terrified animal out of a pit

dug by poachers, or took on board a badly wounded antelope –
there were a number of animals of this kind living with the
elephants. This was real life, it was kindness.

Rob and Elsa learned to assist, far out in the forests, in the
manoeuvring of a panic-stricken beast into the container which
was used to help to redeem the horror of man's cruelty to
wildlife.   Gerald had something of Albert Schweitzer's
"reverence for life".   Elsa and Rob were warned about
venomous snakes. Puff-adders were not uncommon. They were
not to be killed, said Gerald, unless they posed an immediate
threat. He had sometimes trapped one and carried it far out to
the edge of the reserve. Mambas were a different matter, he
said. They were not often seen, but were highly toxic, and if
one turned up near the house he would kill it, though with
regret. One had to concede something to the harsh realities of
evolution. "But," he would add, "I've seen pictures of one of
the most feared venomous snakes, the king cobra. Like many
animals this fearsome creature makes a nest for its young, lays
eggs, perhaps hidden under leaves or brush-wood, and is as
devoted a mother as any human mother is to her babies. If there
is any risk from snakes," he added "take the dogs with you." He
had adopted two half-starved mongrels, found wandering on the
streets of the town, which had been passed on to the vet and so
to him. They were affectionate, and used to the elephants, and
they with them.

"The world," he said, "is marked by lack of respect for life.
In wars, in hunting, in hard-pressed business dealings, in forced
education, above all in the way we treat animals, we show lack
of respect."

Elsa and Rob were now seeing the possibility of an anti-
world world, one where people were able to live in reverse, not
to be afraid of love. When they were under the charitable
regime of Flo and Gerald, sensing the lack of tension, the lack of

aggression, and sometimes the actual gratitude of animals, they seemed to be in contact with a new heaven and new earth. When Dora came to them one day, gently caressing them, they knew they had been accepted into that good kingdom.

(30)

One evening, sensing her partner's tiredness, Elsa got him to bed early. But after an hour or so Rob woke, slipped out of bed, and went to the main living-room, where Gerald was locking up and preparing to retire. Rob asked his friend whether he might stay up a little longer to study the night sky. Gerald gave him the keys and asked him to lock up. "By all means," he said. "It's quite a sight on a fine night. No pollution of the sort we get in cities. Watch out for snakes – take the dogs with you."

Rob went to stand on the verandah, with the dogs at his side. He was immediately aware of an almost audible silence of a kind unknown in the developed world except in the remotest places. Only occasionally the cry of a wild animal broke the stillness.

For a moment or two he felt an overwhelming calm.

He began to remember detail from lessons on astronomy given at school. The class was amazed at first by the concept of the light-year. A light-year is the distance that a speck of light moving at something like 300,000 kilometres per second travels in a year. A light-year is equivalent to 9.5 million million kilometres. The "nearest" star to Earth and so to our own star, the sun, is in the constellation of Centaurus, and is "only" about four light-years from us. Galaxies are collection of millions or billions of stars. Our own galaxy, which we call the Milky Way, is 100,000 light-years in diameter, and Earth, our sun, is a rather insignificant star somewhere near the middle of it. Another "close" galaxy is the great Andromeda Galaxy, 2.2 million light-years away.

The darkness. Had gods really visited the Earth to save it? It had clearly not been saved. All the time there was that low moan of suffering which he knew so well, and sooner or later the Earth would burn up as the sun prepared for its own destruction.

His school class had made a special study of the constellation of Orion, an equatorial star-system which had changed its position, or seemed to, in relation to Rob, but was still visible, with two of its great stars, Rigel, (the giant's leg) about 900 light-years distant, and Betelgeuse, a red supergiant, 310 light-years away. When the pupils used even a small telescope, the whole area of the great mythical giant was ablaze with myriads of stars and star clusters. Even the most sceptical were awed by the Orion Nebula, supposed to represent the belt or club of Orion the hunter. Though another "fuzz" to the naked eye, it was a great cloud of gas and dust with a multiple star at its heart lighting up the surrounding gas.

The Orion nebula is 15 light-years across and lies 1300 light-years away from Earth. Astronomers believe it contains enough gas to make thousands of stars, but it is only one part of the universe in which stars are being born.

Of the millions and trillions of stars being born, attaining star maturity, and later being destroyed, many, perhaps millions or billions, must have given birth to planets. And by the law of averages, millions must, like Earth, support some forms of life.

He suddenly found himself weeping, and knew why. The darkness had fallen, and he knew why. He was back again in that hospital bed, sharing the vision with the bishop holding his dead dog, and the conductor at the close of the symphony. He cried aloud, to a god he did not believe in, to any gods, to blind fate." "No more, no more! Let there be no more like Earth. No more wars, bombings. No more flags, national anthems, practice in killing, all the grisly apparatus of the military. All the waste on death, with one side of this crazy world ready to ruin the other and then ruin the lot. How can one live in the world and be sane?

"Let there be no more grief and sadness in old age, or the sad deaths of children! Let there be no more animals hunted, trapped, caged, skinned, shot, their forests taken from them, slaughtered in agony. Let there be no more evolutions gone wrong, so that their last product is worse than its first. No more politicians deceiving the people. No more men of God, afraid to help the deceived, visionless, churning out the old stale stuff! No more prisons, no more classes, no more races, no more desolate crying children trapped by ignorance and folly."

His eyes swept over the sky, over so many amazing stars, nebulae, and, here and there, just visible, another galaxy.

"Please! No more copies, out there in space, of this rotten miserable speck, mad, cruel, stupid, poisoned, over-crowded." He remembered the remnants - the good on the fringe - relief workers, the kind, good neighbours, the courageous protestors deserted by the bishops. "I know," he cried, "there are good people, but they're outnumbered. Oh, how can the people I love deserve to be stuck in this hell. They have deserved better than to be imprisoned on this pathetic bit of dust. Oh, my God, they have deserved better!"

He was slipping down on to his knees clutching one of the supports of the veranda. Gerald and Flo were running to help, and, distressed beyond measure, his love, Elsa.

She took him to bed holding his trembling body in her arms. Almost at once he fell into, a deep dreamless sleep.

(31)

Not long after sunrise there was a knock at their door. "Sorry," said Gerald, "to wake you so early after a poor night. There are two men attempting to enter the reserve. They've destroyed the lock on the gate by shooting it. We are all roused. "

Two men, each with a rifle, were walking towards the house. Something about them seemed familiar. They were not the two men sent to arrest Rob and Elsa on that peaceful Dales hillside. But they were of the same growth, the same nurturing: slimmish grey men with neat tie and collar, in grey suits this time, and grey inside as well. They were two of the sad thousands and millions who have obeyed orders to do dreadful things to families like their own. The two men advanced to within about fifty yards of the house, and then with voices and faces like those of automata, cold and expressionless, they demanded the return of Rob and Elsa. "They have escaped from an open prison," said one of the men, "and we have to return them. If you won't surrender them we shall have to kill them. They are writing subversive books." (How do they know that, thought Elsa?) "And by their attitude and work they have become a threat to the stability of their nation."

The native boys were now standing behind Gerald and his lady, one of them carrying a rifle. Gerald too held a gun.

Gerald said, "These two new friends of mine are good people. They're doing good work here, saving lives and reducing suffering. If there were more people like them this world would be a happier place."

"Release them!" said one of the strangers, as he and his companion raised their rifles.

"If you shoot them, you must shoot us," said Gerald, "and you too may well die."

A shoot-out now seemed inevitable.

A vision came to Rob. This wasn't the terrible vision of old, but something finer. He was also moved by being able to see something the intruders could not see, movement of animals near the broken entrance to the reserve. But he was also wanting, desperately wanting, to witness to a higher reality than that of the world. Even if these two pitiless automata, solemn and brain-washed, were not equipped to understand it, at least it had to be tried. He stepped forward from behind Gerald's back, where an attempt had been made to conceal him. Gerald and Flo both tried to restrain him, but he broke free, and walked forward towards the two intruders with his arms outstretched, and then paused at a distance, enabling him to look into their eyes. There was no pity, no change in those eyes, the eyes of the hidden side of the Establishment. Something was welling up inside Rob, a desire, almost a joy, to move to a higher level than that of the world.

In a steady voice he said, "I am going to ask you to save us and save yourselves. What is about to happen here would be a microcosm, a symbol, of all that is usual in our world. I mean confrontations, anger, taking sides, victory for one side at the cost of death and destruction. We are about to have a little war. Like all wars it will be ridiculous and vulgar."

"Get on with it!" said one of the men. "Give yourselves up, or we will shoot."

Elsa had run forward and was standing close to Rob, who went on, "Like the animals here, we all have precious, marvellously-constructed bodies. All our mothers will have gone through pain and joy many years ago to bring us into the world. To shoot or kill anything is a betrayal of all that. And," he added, looking again into the middle distance, "I think you'll need our help to be saved."

The two men looked round. Elephants, forming a kind of horse-shoe pattern, were narrowing the escape route from the reserve. At the broken gate itself Dora and one or two of the larger elephants were keeping guard.

"If you shoot us," said Gerald, "the animals here, who love us, will kill you before you can escape."

The two men conferred anxiously.

"I think I should add," said Gerald, "that we should abandon our weapons. The elephants will not let you through if they see guns. Many of them have known guns in their time."

As if accepting the strange spiritual-waveband on which they were operating, Gerald moved forward and, advancing a little beyond Rob and Elsa, placed his gun on the ground in front of the two strangers. "I agree with my friend," he said, "let us do better than the world." Then, with a touch of hard common-sense, "Don't think you can get out any other way. It's a long way to the other exit and we're now almost ringed round. Put down your weapons with mine."

Terrified of what they now saw behind them, the government servants turned, and dropped their rifles, and began to half-run, half-walk towards the broken gate. There was a small space left in the gateway between, on the one side, a small group of elephants with their young, and on the other side the great bulk of Dora, her body swaying from side to side, her trunk raised, but not in love. In abject terror the intruders walked through the narrow gap left to them, almost under Dora's feet, and then they were gone into the forest.

For moment everything seemed to stand still as in a kind of tableau. And then everyone and everybody began to relax, and the elephants began to disperse.

Rob and Elsa walked forward over the great expanse of green towards the gate. When they were about half-way, they stopped, because Dora was coming towards them. She stopped too, in the middle of that oasis of peace, letting her trunk rest, then curl, around the shoulders of her two friends. Without a thought, Rob and Elsa knelt down before her. Dora stood above them, in protective love.

www.ingramcontent.com/pod-product-compliance
Lightning Source LLC
Chambersburg PA
CBHW030524260626
47157CB00005B/1872